Look for these other
Dog Lover's Mysteries
by Melissa Cleary!

A TAIL OF TWO MURDERS

Jackie finds a beautiful dog with a bullet wound
in his leg . . . and, not much later, the dead body of
her boss at the Rodgers U. film department. The
cunning canine may be a big help in solving the
crime . . .

DOG COLLAR CRIME

Dog trainer and basset hound devotee Mel
Sweeten is killed with a choke collar . . . and Jackie
and Jake have to dig up the facts to find out who-
dunit . . .

HOUNDED TO DEATH

Mayoral hopeful Morton Slake has the morals
of an alley cat—but when his girlfriend is found
dead, Jackie and Jake prove that every dog has his
day . . .

SKULL AND DOG BONES

MELISSA CLEARY

BERKLEY PRIME CRIME, NEW YORK

SKULL AND DOG BONES

A Berkley Prime Crime Book / published by arrangement with the author

PRINTING HISTORY
Jove edition / January 1994
Berkley Prime Crime edition / February 1994

ISBN: 0-425-14541-7

Berkley Prime Crime Books are published
by The Berkley Publishing Group,
200 Madison Avenue, New York, New York 10016.
The name BERKLEY PRIME CRIME and the
BERKLEY PRIME CRIME
design are trademarks belonging to Berkley Publishing Corporation.

PRINTED IN THE UNITED STATES OF AMERICA

10   9   8   7   6   5   4   3

For D.

The once-elegant Spanish rococo house stood empty. It was just a matter of time before an Arab potentate bought the property and destroyed the former film director's house in order to "ground down and build up" a grander property on the same valuable plot of land.

The bungalow in the back still held a table where Georgiana Bowman had refashioned scripts into something she could shoot on the tiny budgets the studios offered her. The bedrooms upstairs still contained some of the Bowman furniture, once considered worthy of fashion spreads in *Home Beautiful*. The closets still held the tailored, mannish suits that Bowman wore on the set and at the few studio affairs she attended. The swimming pool, drained after the accident, still existed beneath the leaves from some fifty summers. Everything in Georgiana Bowman's house existed as if she were still out there somewhere, ready to come back and resume her life as Hollywood's first female director. But although many people suspected, only one man knew for sure that this would never be.

CHAPTER 1

The body on the morgue slab showed no sign of having been in a movie star's swimming pool for six hours. The sheet covering the tall, well-built male form wasn't even damp. A tag on the left great toe of the corpse was only partly visible. You could see the "Joe" but nothing else. If this scene had been left in the final print of *Sunset Boulevard* as director Billy Wilder had intended, Jackie Walsh speculated, listening to William Holden's voice start into the opening narration, they would have had to cut in an insert tag with the character's full name.

Jackie let the shot continue until the camera was about to focus on the face of Gloria Swanson on the front page of the newspaper on the coroner's desk. Then, with an enormous feeling of relief, Jackie stopped her off-line recorder and reached for the next tape.

Only three more sequences and she would be done.

The idea she had, to quiz her Film History 101 students by putting together a reel of clips that never got into the feature they were shot for (instead ending up on the cutting-room floor), had been a good one. Unfortunately, it was only when the slim, intense college professor started going through the hundreds of tapes she had collected during her Hollywood days plus another big box she had gotten from the university's Philip Barger Film Library that Jackie realized that most of the excised film clips involved the stars of the movie in distinctive costumes or settings that easily gave away the picture.

One didn't have to be an avid film buff to guess that the colorfully costumed Judy Garland, Ray Bolger, and Buddy Ebsen singing "The Jitterbug" came from *The Wizard of Oz,* or that a clip showing Kevin Costner, in jeans and long hair, kibitzing with William Hurt and Jeff Goldblum must have come from *The Big Chill.* Unfortunately, Jackie had already announced the quiz and now had to follow through with it.

When Jake came in to disturb her reverie, Jackie was almost grateful for the interruption.

The large Alsatian padded into the little office Jackie had carved out of a section of her living room and immediately tried to squeeze his tightly muscled body and massive head between the neatly stacked scripts and weekly issues of *Variety* that Jackie kept near her workout mat in the corner.

"Hi, Jake. What's up, boy?"

The answer to why Jake had decided to abandon his comfortable bed under the kitchen table and pay a visit came quickly as the all-too-familiar sound of bagpipes, drum machines, and Irish-accented rap singing assaulted their ears.

"Peter!" Jackie called out.

Jackie's eleven-year-old son, looking as he usually did on summer evenings when he didn't have hockey practice—as if he had been sleeping on the floor—stuck his head in the doorway. "Yes, Mom?"

"I thought," Jackie said, making an effort to stay calm, "we agreed if you wanted to listen to that tape you would use your Walkman."

"Sorry!" Peter vanished and Jackie got up to stretch.

Jake, grateful to his mistress for having caused the awful music to stop, decided he would do the same, and gave himself a good shake in the bargain.

"Okay, boy," Jackie promised. "We'll take that walk in about twenty minutes. I promise."

Jake nodded happily and laid back down. Although he had been one of the toughest and meanest patrol dogs during his sojourn on the Palmer police force, Jake was always agreeable with his adopted family. The most the big dog would ever show when Jackie or Peter let him down was a sorrowful look of disappointment.

"One more clip," the big dog's mistress groaned to herself. Finally, deciding on a short sequence showing Frank Sinatra as Billy Bigelow in *Carousel,* Jackie rolled her neck and prepared to sit her stiff, sore body back down at the off-line recorder. She had not been getting enough exercise lately since the Rodgers University swim team was monopolizing the gymnasium swimming pool during the early A.M. hours when she had formerly done her daily half mile. Figuring her concentration was already broken, Jackie walked over to her exercise mat and debated whether to do a brisk ten-minute aerobics workout or just stretch out a bit with a few minutes of yoga. Before she could choose, Peter interrupted her again.

"Mom!"

"What, honey?" Jackie turned and saw her son walking through the living room toward her, wearing earphones and holding an almost-new Walkman out to her.

"This doesn't work. I need a new one."

Jackie walked over and tousled her boy's thick curls. Hoping to avoid dipping into her already overtaxed monthly budget, she asked her son, "Did you drop it?"

"No."

"What about the batteries?"

Peter shifted back and forth on one foot impatiently. "It's got batteries."

Jackie put her hands on her son's shoulders to get him to stop. "Did you remember to put them in the recharger last night, like I told you?"

"I think maybe I might've forgot."

"Well, then," Jackie said, nodding. "I think maybe your batteries might be dead."

"Oh."

Jackie pulled her groaning son into a hug. "Isn't it time you got a haircut?"

Peter shrugged. "How can I listen to my tape when we don't have any batteries?"

"Put the batteries in the recharger now," Jackie instructed. "You can put the stereo back on for a few minutes when I walk Jake."

"Can't I go with you?"

"No, you have homework to do. When I get home, you're going to bed."

Peter reacted with outrage and horror. "If you're not going to go right away, then I can't listen to my tape. I can't draw if I can't listen to my tape."

Jackie gave her son a narrow look. "Peter, you listen to that tape all day long—at home, at art school, your coach lets you play it at practice—you don't have to listen to it every minute of every day."

"I like it!" Peter wailed.

"I like Bernard Herrmann, but I don't play *Psycho* every day and drive you and Jake crazy!"

Peter shrugged again and rolled his eyes. Jackie and her son were going through a mildly rocky passage at present. Clearly he was missing his father.

"What about Mike?" Peter demanded. "Is he coming by tonight?"

"Maybe this weekend," Jackie responded.

Peter tugged open the top drawer of Jackie's black file cabinet so he could have something to lean on. "We never see him anymore."

"We see him plenty," Jackie responded patiently, "but he's working and so am I."

"You weren't working," Peter accused. "You were going to stand on your head."

"You got it. Now if you'll excuse me." Jackie cinched her black cloth belt tighter so that her dark sweatshirt top would not flop over her head, went down to all fours, quickly pulled her knees onto her elbows, and extended to a full headstand. Jake, as always, stood at alert. He was not yet used to upside-down mistresses.

"Can I ask you one more thing?" Peter asked, after slamming the file cabinet drawer shut.

"Make it a quick one," Jackie responded, feeling the blood rushing to her head.

"Will you bring me back some chocolate peanut butter ice cream?"

"Would you settle for a fruit pop?"

"Not diet."

"Diet," Jackie said firmly.

Peter got enough exercise to keep his weight down, but even at the relatively early age of eleven, he was showing unmistakable signs of developing his father's potbelly. Jackie was determined to get him through his teens in as good a condition as possible.

"Never mind, then!" Peter replied angrily. "Just skip it!"

As her son departed in a huff, Jackie sighed and blew a wisp of her long black hair out of her eyes. She knew from experience that the batteries would not now make their way into the recharger—knew also that Black 47 would be blaring from the stereo again any second.

Then, as if on cue, the music she had begun to regard with the same sort of loathing and fascination her father had held for Lou Christie and Frankie Valli came on again—louder than before.

Jackie sighed, then giggled, the laugh almost causing her to lose her balance. Catching herself just in time, she thought, *It never gets any easier, does it?*

Spreading her legs briefly, giving herself a long stretch down the length of her spine, Jackie then stopped to reflect briefly on how she had been as a teenager.

Jackie's mother, Frances, like Jackie for many years, had simply been a homemaker. Pete, Jackie's father, had been a writer (of the popular fifties television show *Tales of Justice,* among other shows) and a film professor who sometimes worked at home. Because Pete was the head of the then small Communications Studies department, he was always bringing home all sorts of administrative work in addition

to his professional writing chores. Although he loved his
daughter and tried to keep calm when she interrupted him,
John Peter Costello was not above locking his loved ones
out when the crunch was on. For being a little kinder and
more patient with her son's interruptions, Jackie was now
being made to pay the price.

All of a sudden, Jackie's musings were interrupted by a
harsh teenage voice. "Mom!"

"What is it?" Jackie responded.

"Telephone!" Peter then popped into the doorway carrying
the cellular phone. "You want it down there?"

Jackie smiled briefly and rolled out, ending somewhat
unsteadily back on her feet. "Thanks, anyway." She took
the phone and carried it back over to her desk. "Hello?"

"Hello, Jackie Costello?" It was the voice of a man her
father's age, which she could not immediately place.

"It's Jackie Walsh, now," Jackie replied carefully.

"Married another Irishman, eh?"

"Actually, I'm divorced. I'm sorry, do I . . . ?"

"I'm an old friend of Pete's," the voice responded. "Maybe you remember him talking about me, Ralph Perrin . . . ?"

Jackie searched her memory for the name. Certainly he
knew her father at least slightly if he called him "Pete." Professionally her dad was always J.P. and people who did not
know him well called him John, which he hated. "I'm sorry,"
she responded. "I'm afraid it doesn't ring any bells."

"Well, Jackie . . . if I may . . . ?"

"Of course."

"I have a request of you," the voice on the phone continued. "I know it's a lot to ask from someone you don't
know from Adam, but I've got a book I wrote about the old
motion picture director Georgiana Bowman."

"Really?" Jackie didn't often think of Georgiana Bowman,
but when she did she often wondered why there had not been
at least one biography of the fairly colorful motion picture
pioneer.

"Yeah. It's based on some interviews with her done out here in California."

Jackie was surprised again, although she did not interrupt. Could he mean recent interviews? Was Georgiana Bowman really still alive? Her heyday was the twenties and thirties; this would make her at least eighty something and very likely older.

"It's a good book," the warm voice on the other end continued, "but it's not very long, and the paperback companies tell me she's just too obscure for mass market."

"I'm afraid that's probably true," Jackie confirmed. "I teach Film History at the college here and I'm surprised at the Hollywood pioneers my students don't know. I mentioned Cecil B. DeMille last week and you should have seen the blank looks."

"There you go," the telephone voice responded. "Anyway, at this point I'd be happy to make what little I can and to see the thing in print, even if it was just a small imprint through your college."

Jackie nodded at that. Jonathan Kersch, the deputy department chairman and titular head of the Rodgers University Publishing Press, was always on the lookout for titles for both their "Women in Film" and "American Directors" series. If this book really covered Georgiana Bowman's career and featured interviews with the lady herself it would be perfect, since the pioneer director's life could fit into either category.

"Would you mind taking a look, if I sent you the manuscript?" the voice resumed. "It's still a little rough, and I haven't rounded up much in the way of pictures, but if you thought it was worth pursuing, it'd be a real kick in the pants for me to do a final draft and submit it."

"I'd be happy to look at the book, er . . ."

"Ralph! Listen, I really appreciate it. Where should I send it?"

Jackie started to give the man her home address, but then something stopped her. "Just send it to me care of Rodgers

University, Communications Studies, room 419."

"Okay, great! And thanks. Maybe we can get together for a cup of coffee after you take a look through her. What do you say? Exchange a few stories about your old man?"

Jackie considered for a moment, then a wave of nostalgia whipped through her and she decided.

"I'd like that . . . Ralph."

"Okay. I'll send it out to you right away. Ciao."

Jackie hung up the phone slowly, absently reaching out toward Jake at the same time. The large Alsatian padded over to his mistress's side and pushed up against her. Jake was always happy for a hug, understanding that in this case, this was something Jackie needed to do too. She ran her fingers through his thick brown and black hair, telling her able assistant, "Why do I have the feeling I am about to get into trouble again, Jake?"

Not having an answer, the big dog just smiled.

CHAPTER 2

The Communications Studies bulletin board in the Faculty Lounge at Longacre Center was festooned with offers for tickets to various parts of the country—Los Angeles; New York; Orlando, Florida.

"The stuff dreams are made of," Jackie lisped to herself as if a Bogart character. Shaking her head, she leafed through the mail that had been stuck in her pigeonhole. The airlines were having a fare war again and people were snapping up tickets to places all over the country. Once they got the tickets these same people were either trying to turn them over at a profit, or were desperately trying to unload them after they realized that they weren't able to get the time off or that they would not be able to afford the hotels and meals that would have to be bought after they had cheaply flown somewhere.

Jackie herself had not had a vacation in some time, and could certainly use one. She was fumbling through her black leather fannie pack for her office key when a peremptory voice behind her blared out, "Ms. Walsh!"

Startled, the drowsy film instructor turned around to see the Teutonic department secretary, Polly Merton, glaring at her from the other end of the corridor. "Uh, yes?"

Ms. Merton crossed her arms and spat out, "I've been waiting since nine o'clock to speak with you."

Jackie frowned at the woman. Polly Merton seemed to see things the way she dressed, in black and white.

"I'm terribly sorry, Polly. I let my TA give the quiz this morning so I could prepare for my lab."

Miss Merton nodded skeptically, as if reluctantly swallowing a preposterous tissue of lies. "Might I have a word with you, *Miss* Walsh?"

"Sure." Jackie opened her door and gestured as if to invite the blond secretary into her small cubicle.

"At my desk please," Miss Merton responded tightly.

"I'll be right . . . in," Jackie told the sound of departing footsteps.

"Somebody's in trouble," sang out Mark Freeman, the animated little animation instructor, as he emerged from the next cubicle with his breakfast.

Jackie fixed a baleful "I haven't had my coffee yet—so watch it" look on the brash Mr. Freeman and remarked coolly, "Is an overstuffed donut really the best choice, Mark, when you're trying to lose weight?"

Chastened, Mark set his donut inside on his desk and held up his arms like a battered fighter. "Okay, *no mas. No mas.* Are you expecting a call from somebody?"

Jackie shook her head.

"Oh. No biggie, but your phone's been ringing on and off all morning."

"Okay, thanks." Jackie went into her cubicle, a small cramped little corner office that she tried to make her own with a wide assortment of potted cacti, framed pictures, and a large poster of Mae West. Flicking on her desk light, Jackie set her heavy blue shoulder bag full of videotapes down on the small counterdesk and quickly looked at the screen of her personal computer to see if the electronic mail icon was flashing. No. No messages there.

Jackie switched on the one-cup coffee maker her policeman-friend Michael McGowan had gotten her for Christmas. If Eva Braun Merton was mad at her, Jackie was going to need all the caffeine fortification she could get.

The dark-haired film instructor then reached for her phone and dialed her own home number. She pushed the pound button, then her own code, and waited to hear if there were any messages on her answering machine. No. Whoever had been trying to call her here had apparently not called her at home. Jackie hung up and poured an Almost Sugar into her coffee.

What was it now? she wondered. Something with her teaching assistant, in all probability. Suki Tonawanka was a very sweet, very intelligent young lady but somehow every-thing she did annoyed Perfect Polly Merton. If, for instance, Polly had discovered that Jackie had given Suki a copy of her cubicle key, this would be a terrible bone of contention.

The faculty cubicle keys in the new system all opened the walk-in supply closet in the chairman's office (no longer under the capable Miss Merton's personal supervision), the rest rooms, and several video supply closets. Officially, Com. Study teaching assistants were supposed to go to Polly Merton whenever they wanted to get into the cubicles when the instructors they worked with were not around. This was not a very effective system under any circumstances, and with a tyrant like Polly Merton using her limited power to drive the TAs crazy, it had not worked at all. Therefore, each of the film instructors ended up doing what Jackie had done—they either inconvenienced themselves by giving their TA their own key and then worried about getting it back, or they went to a locksmith off campus and had the key illegally duplicated.

Sighing at the office politics that made an otherwise pleas-ant job a chore, Jackie took another long hit off her coffee. She then sat down to write an electronic message to Deputy Chairman Kersch about Ralph Perrin's book proposal.

When Jackie finally entered the chairman's outer office, a neat antiseptic area that had been designed by the department secretary to look like a dentist's waiting room, Polly Merton was standing in her version of the military "Parade Rest" stance.

"Ms. Walsh."

"Yes, Ms. Merton. How can I help you?" Jackie expected Perfect Polly to launch into a tirade about keys that would end in her usual threat, which was to get the odious head of college security, Walter Hopfelt, to change all the locks "this very day." So confident was Jackie that this was going to happen that when Polly threw her a curve by instead spending several moments checking out her wardrobe, the young film instructor was terribly discomfited.

"Those pants," Ms. Merton said.

Jackie looked down at one of the several pairs of black pull-on gabardine slacks she practically lived in on teaching days. "Yes?"

"Where did you get them?"

Jackie's brain raced. Was she now going to accuse her of stealing clothing from other teachers' cubicles? "Mail order."

"European?" Miss Merton inquired.

"A New York company," Jackie replied.

"I'm referring to the designer."

"Oh." Jackie had the feeling that the conversation was shortly leading to unpleasantness, but she was willing to oblige with small talk as long as Ms. Merton was. "He's Yugoslavian, I believe. Lives in Virginia now. At least that's what I read in *Vanity Fair*."

"Were you expecting a fax?"

Jackie's head reeled trying to find the connection. "I . . . uh . . ."

"You must have been," Miss Merton announced, "since it is addressed to *you*!" With what amounted to a hiss, Polly Merton moved to one side, revealing the poor, overworked Longacre fax machine and a stack of printed paper.

"I have been *forced*"—Miss Merton squeezed out each word as if straining to hold back the memory of recent unspeakable horrors—"to fill the paper tray . . . *three* times!"

"I'm sorry," Jackie said automatically.

Clearly not considering Jackie's tone to be nearly contrite enough, Miss Merton finally let loose the icy torrent of words Jackie had been expecting. "The *new* Department of *Communications* fax machine was *designed* for communiqués between traveling faculty and *administrators*. *Personal* faxes may be *tolerated* under *certain* conditions, approved in *advance,* in *writing,* by the *chairman.* It should be *obvious* that an expensive, er, *delicate* device such as *this* one is not designed for *heavy* use. Especially the receipt of *two hundred and twenty pages* of manuscript. What could you have been *thinking,* Ms. Walsh?"

"I apologize again, Miss Merton," Jackie responded, moving closer to the pile of pages, "that the department fax machine was so cruelly abused. But I certainly didn't arrange for anything like this. Are you sure it's for me? Maybe they put my name on it by mistake."

"There was no mistake, Miss Walsh," Perfect Polly replied with a smile that would chill antifreeze. "Not on my part, anyway. Now, Chairman Quest would like to see you. Immediately."

Jackie tried hard not to wince as Miss Merton handed her the manuscript and turned off the printer with a loud snap. "Thank you."

The office of the chairman, was, as always, dazzling. Ivor Quest, one of the great directors in American film history, had agreed, after the celebrated departures of the last two Communications department chairpeople, to take over the position. The announcement had been made largely to satisfy Stuart Goodwillie, who at that time was still a pharmaceutical billionaire and the university's largest patron.

As one might suspect, Quest had taken the job under the understanding that it would be a largely ceremonial title and that the actual running of the department would be done by Jonathan Kersch, an instructor in the department with a background in arts administration, who would be promoted to deputy chairman.

Away in Hollywood, New York, or Europe at least three months of the term and most of the summer, Quest had

brought a great deal of favorable publicity to the school,
a much-needed commodity after a series of unfortunate
incidents had rocked the university. Quest had also been
very instrumental in bringing money to the school from
his Hollywood sources. It was money that replaced the
now-gone-forever federal funds and the alternately generous
and impecunious strings-attached grants that had once come
from Stuart Goodwillie. What this meant to the university
was that the Communications School was, for the first time
in recent memory, relatively independent to follow its own
agenda.

"Miss Walsh!" Chairman Quest beamed upon seeing her
enter. "How delightful of you to stop in. Please, have a
seat."

Jackie sank into a visitor's chair that cost more than
most compact cars and started, "Chairman Quest, I'd like
to explain . . ."

Quest waved the words away and announced, "These
ancient ears are quite deaf to anyone who addresses me as
anything but 'Ivor.' "

The charming English-born director was impeccably
dressed in the sort of summer whites one would expect
to see in the English colony area of Jamaica. Unlike
the new-style Hollywood moguls who believed in dress-
ing like gangsters, with pounds of expensive jewelry to
match, Ivor Quest wore nothing he did not have to wear.
Rolex watches, for instance, were useless to a man like
Ivor Quest. What did he care, after all, for what time
it was?

In fact, Ivor Quest had made great use of the time he had
spent as the Rodgers University Department of Communications chairman. His first decision as chairman had been
to sell the film rights of the Kestral Trilogy to the new
British Television Network at a handsome profit. "Let *them*
resolve the copyright difficulties," he had decreed. Next,
Quest had taken it upon himself to personally find posi-
tions in the film industry for the most successful graduates

of the Film program. Students like Nadia Pitts were now comfortably ensconced in jobs that they could not have hoped to land for a minimum of another five years in the usual circumstances.

Then Quest had completely redecorated his office, at his own expense, hiring a world-class decorator who was rumored to be a former lover of the great director. Antoine of Paris had turned the chairman's office into a dwelling at once reminiscent of San Simeon and the deck of the Starship *Enterprise*. Jackie was dazzled to see Quest put his sandaled feet up on a desk that had been photographed for the cover of *Art Deco Furniture,* a runaway best-selling coffee-table book.

Trying to put all this aside, Jackie resumed, "Anyway, Ivor, I just want to—"

Quest interrupted her at once, "As you know, Jacqueline— if I may address you so?"

Jackie nodded at once.

"I have spent the last fifty years of my life in the land of wretched excess." As if to prove the point, Quest pointed to the glass display shelves lining the office walls holding literally hundreds of pictures and souvenirs, including two Academy Award statuettes that the always charming Ivor had confided to the faculty staff were cheap plated plaster duplicates of the originals, which had been safely locked away in a London vault.

"The question, therefore, of how many pages you have had faxed to you is so far beneath my notice, it might as well not even exist."

"Thank you," Jackie said, brushing back the dark curls from her forehead with a great sigh of relief. "Still . . ."

"The only way you could possibly offend me," Quest continued, "is to continue to dwell on such an utterly mundane matter." As if to hammer home the point, the department chairman swiveled in a chair that had cost a little more than a year's tuition to the school, to admire the view from his newly installed bay window. "What an utterly gorgeous afternoon. I can't tell you how I envy you all for living here all year round."

"I'm sure there are at least a few people on campus who would trade places with you."

Quest swiveled back. "The bane of our existence. We all of us envy the life we do not lead. How are you, Jacqueline? What a pretty outfit! Zoran?"

Jackie nodded.

"The curse of doing costume pictures. I was never able to use the brilliant clothes of a modern designer." Quest then steepled his fingers. "You are wondering why I asked you in, of course."

Jackie nodded.

"My training as an executive," Quest began, instinctively moving into his light, "if you can call it that, has taught me, lo these many moons, to always delegate the unpleasant business of breaking bad news to an associate. This task has been given to Mr. Kersch more than once, I'm afraid."

Jackie nodded again. She had heard how upset Stuart Goodwillie had been when Jonathan Kersch had been forced to tell him that his handpicked successor to the job of Film department chairman had decided that the job of producing a major motion picture with Film department students and local Palmer community playhouse technicians was preposterous.

"I reserve for myself of course"—Quest smiled his "best false teeth in Hollywood" smile again—"the pleasure of personally dispensing *good* news."

"Oh?"

Quest twisted his features into a look of pious concern. "Miss Merton, I am afraid, is leaving us. I've persuaded the English department to take her as a transfer. The subtraction of her not-inconsiderable salary and the infusion of some new capital into our department will allow us to replace her, eventually, with two full-time secretaries and two part-time secretaries. We will labor mightily to find more congenial souls."

Jackie bit her lip to keep from cheering aloud. And the day had started out so badly.

"Perhaps you didn't hear me, Jacqueline."

"Oh, no," Jackie managed to get out. "That's wonderful."

"I'm glad you think so." Quest smiled with his eyes. "I must compliment you on your restraint. When I mentioned my decision to Yelena Gruber she embraced me and danced a jig on my rug. Fred Jackson streaked out the door telling me he'd be back in five minutes with a case of champagne."

Jackie smiled, knowing Quest was probably exaggerating the reactions of the temperamental Hungarian acting instructress and the bearded bon vivant cinematography instructor, but enjoying the images just the same.

"I think it is . . . very good news, Ivor," Jackie said finally. "I just don't want to be mean."

"Admirable, Miss Walsh," Quest approved in a loud voice. "Entirely admirable, but quite unnecessary, I assure you. If Miss Merton were being dismissed to live on the streets it would be one thing."

"She'd make out," Jackie said confidently. "In no time she'd have cornered the market on refundable cans."

"Exactly." Quest beamed. "But instead she will go to Literature, which is in dire need of reorganization."

"That's what the book reviewer on the Palmer *Herald* is always saying."

Jackie referred to the inestimable Ms. Scott, who, although she had known Jackie her entire life, had never let Jackie call her Jean. Though she'd been a fixture in her parents' apartment when she was growing up, Jackie hadn't seen Ms. Scott since the formidable woman had come to her wedding and proposed the majority of the toasts that the father of the bride was too inebriated to deliver. They were no longer in touch, but Jackie still read Jean Scott's column in the Monday, Wednesday, and Sunday *Herald,* just to relish the sound of her voice. Ms. Scott wrote the way she talked, and Ms. Scott did not like modern novels.

"Touché," Quest responded with insincere appreciation. Clearly he was preoccupied. "May I interest you, Ms. Walsh," the director asked as he jumped to his feet and crossed quickly to the rolling wet bar that had replaced the late Chairman Barger's credenza, "in a spritzer?"

"Is that with alcohol?" Jackie asked.

"It could be." The department chairman's artificially tanned hand settled on a marbled glass decanter that he held briefly aloft so Jackie could see it. "I make my own with a teaspoon of this disgustingly sweet loganberry extract in a large tumbler of icy seltzer."

"That sounds lovely,"

"Good. You'll remind me, when I complete my chemical experiments, of what we were speaking."

"Literature," Jackie said absently.

"No, the Literature department," Quest corrected.

"And their secretarial situation."

"Which you're familiar with?" Quest queried, handing Jackie her drink.

"Somewhat," she admitted. Actually Jackie was more than somewhat familiar with the miserable mess that had existed in the Rodgers Fine Arts Literature program since she had been a student.

The chairman, Algernon Foreman, a sweet, warm dumpling of a man resembling the old character actor S. Z. "Cuddles" Sakal, had been more than adequate in teaching, laying out an exacting curriculum and attracting intelligent, capable, much-published professors. He had been a disaster when it came to hiring secretarial help, though. Almost from the very start of his tenure, the department office had been manned by a series of cute, bubbly young girls, just out of secretarial school, who would quickly learn that their boss cared nothing about what they did as long as they showed up for work and treated everyone pleasantly.

You could seldom get through to anyone in Literature, although year after year they added more telephone lines, because the secretaries were forever on the phone making personal calls. The filing system was designed to accommodate secretaries who could not spell and did not like to chance chipping a nail rummaging through file cabinets. They would take each and every paper that came into the office and put it into a brand-new manila file folder and then, writing what was by this time a six or seven digit number on the outside, the folders would be placed in any one of several hundred open paper boxes lying on the floors of every room, office, and corridor. When the boxes became unmanageable the secretaries would simply call the maintenance men to throw away the ten or twenty boxes that seemed to be the oldest ones.

And so it would go.

Computers had been added to help the problem, but the same haphazard filing methods had just been transferred intact to the new electronic system. Currently, Jackie had heard, the Literature computer system was slowed to a near standstill, burdened with thousands of consecutively numbered computer files, which would eventually be filed off onto diskettes, which then would be tossed into empty boxes until the new inadequate system would entirely replace the old.

Jackie's musings were interrupted as the chairman finished his drink and laid his glass down with a click on a ceramic coaster featuring a major Aztec deity. "So . . . you are familiar with how desperately they need Miss Merton's organizational skills."

"It may kill her."

"In which case the generous university insurance plan will promptly compensate her heirs."

Jackie and Quest exchanged smiles.

At the same time the conversation between Jackie and her chairman was going on, just outside of town, in his comfortable suburban Kingswood home, Cosmo Gordon, the Canadian-born medical examiner of Palmer, looked at his mirrored image and groaned to his wife, "What are the dry cleaners doing to my tuxedo?"

Nancy Gordon, a lovely former Miss Puerto Rico, patted her husband's paunch and commented, "Well, they're not sewing extra material into the waistband, if that's what you mean. Katharina-Elena's recital is next week. That means you're going to have to wear that suit again, you know."

"Terrific!" Cosmo pulled on his trousers several times, trying to get them into a position where they wouldn't bind. "I can't understand how this could have happened."

"Do you think it could have been all those cheeseburgers at the Juniper Tavern, dear?"

"No, I think it's all these high-calorie meals you make for us here."

Nancy came over and put her arms around her husband's neck. "You are still very handsome, Cosmo."

"You're a storyteller, Nancy. I'm an old man and look it. You look like my daughter when we go to these functions. And speaking of which, why can't Kathy-Elaine come with us today? She knows how much this means to Xenia."

The Gordons were fixing to attend a memorial service for Matthew Dugan, a former policeman, much decorated, whom Cosmo had befriended in his last years. Nancy didn't let on, but she didn't much like the clingy Mrs. Dugan.

"Cosmo, Katharina-Elena didn't know Matt's family. She has her studies."

"All right, all right," Cosmo grouched. "Are you sure you want to go? You only met Xenia and the children one time yourself."

"I want to go, my husband." Elena kissed the balding, red-faced physician on the cheek. "I'm ready. Are you?"

"Just have to find my Masonic cufflinks," Gordon wheezed. "Go on downstairs. Start turning things off. I promised we'd get there early and help her seat people."

"All right." Nancy patted Cosmo's stomach and walked toward the door.

"You look very nice in that dress, by the way," Cosmo called after her. Then, as soon as his smiling wife left the room, he unbuttoned the clasp on his pants below the cummerbund. Seeing the widow and children of his murdered friend would be hard enough.

At the same time, in the chairman's office at the Longacre Center, Chairman Quest continued to explain the upcoming changes to Jackie.

"While Miss Merton may be just what Literature needs, our requirements are different. We are adding faculty, you will be happy to hear, Jacqueline."

Jackie smiled widely. "That is good news."

"Indeed it is!" Quest exclaimed, slapping his palm against his glass-topped desk for emphasis. "And when the top-floor computer people finally complete their move to the MicroElectronics Building we can nab that space for new classrooms. Then, at long last, we will *finally* be able to use the entire first floor for the faculty."

"Really?"

"I wouldn't run down to the decorator's yet," Quest cautioned with a smile. "You know how long these things take. But we hope to add offices for the senior staff, of course, and a decent faculty lounge."

"Where?"

"Ms. Green's old office suite," Quest replied quickly, as if expecting an argument. "Since she is no longer with us, we will completely refurbish it into a lounge. The old lounge will house our videotape and videodisc library, which I hope to expand greatly."

Jackie's head just whirled with happiness. "This all sounds so wonderful."

"I think so." Quest smiled. "We won't be able to compete with the southern California or New York City schools yet, but it will make some sort of feature film or television production at least possible in the future. And, the hope is, we will attract both matriculating students and perhaps graduate students or return-to-schoolers anxious to brush up or learn anew some part of our Communications Skills curriculum."

"Can we . . . handle it?"

"With our current staff?" Quest clasped at his breast in mock surprise and indignation. "My word, no. I agree with those of you who felt your old course burdens were intolerable." The department chairman then leaned forward and, with a great sweep of his hand, started to paint the future for Jackie. "I see the staff doubling within two years, Jacqueline. That's why I've been calling each of you separately to explain what we anticipate. I'll have a complete package for each of you at the staff meeting on Thursday—but I can tell you now, specifically, that we will be able to accommodate the suggestions you outlined in your May memo."

"Really?" Jackie thought back to the long, detailed memo she had written Quest care of his Berkeley, California, office. In the memo, which had detailed the procedures instituted during the Barger and Green administrations, she had complained at length, and in detail, about the crazy scheduling that had caused her and fellow faculty, now short two full-time instructors, to work seven days a week and cover for each other, teaching courses they had little or no familiarity with at a moment's notice. The teaching assistants, making little more than pocket change, had already started walking out in droves and the students, fed up with the enormous classes and constant cancellations or substitutions of movies for labs and lectures, were transferring out in record numbers. Jackie had therefore demanded that the classes be cut in half, which logically meant hiring twice as many instructors. This also meant that floaters, who would be able to pinch-hit for at least three or four of the instructors, would have to be put on retainer and that teaching assistants would have to be given free or heavily subsidized housing and a salary at least commensurate with the minimum wage. In truth, Jackie would have settled to have at least some of her gripes answered. She was amazed to hear that Quest was willing to address every one of them.

"Really and truly, Jacqueline. You seem astounded."

"Thunderstruck."

"How gratifying to know I can still move the earth beneath an attractive young woman." Quest raised an eyebrow with perfect comic timing.

Jackie obliged with her fullest laugh.

"This isn't exactly an act of charity," the department chairman explained. "Or solely to impress the more exquisitely impressionable members of my staff. The truth is, I plan to take this chairmanship seriously. Would I rather run a studio than a Communications Studies department in a Midwest university? Well, obviously. But even in the unlikely event I were offered such an opportunity now, after being passed over for so many years, it really is at long last too late for me. They want bankers and international financiers to head their companies now. To these creatures movies are simply celluloid comic books. They not only do not strive for quality films, but when presented with one on a sterling silver platter they do their very best to destroy them—for if one fishcake in a frozen package tastes delicious, then you must explain to the consumer why the other nineteen taste like cardboard. You must actually then treat your fishcake buyers as people with human needs for sustenance instead of squealing pigs who can be fattened up eating other people's garbage." Quest's voice faded.

"The last thing anyone in Hollywood wants to hear from me are stories of the old days. Here in your lovely university"—Quest waved his hands elegantly all around him—"they want to hear nothing else. So"—the chairman's voice then returned to its normal pitch and vigor—"this is where I will make my stand, my dear. And I will make it as comfortable a bunker for the lot of us as I can possibly manage. I hope you don't consider me completely trivial and vain."

"I think you're wonderful." Jackie smiled.

"The very answer I was looking for!" Quest winked at her "Now, if you'll excuse me, I will call in the next staff member and start the whole delightful episode of making their up-to-now dreary day bright all over again."

Jackie took her cue to stand. Quest stood with her and they solemnly shook hands.

"Well," Jackie said, smiling, "you certainly have done that for me. Thank you."

"You are very welcome indeed," Quest replied. "Enjoy your reading."

"Beg pardon?" Jackie was momentarily disoriented.

"Your million-dollar manuscript," Quest reminded her, pointing to the untidy stack of faxed pages near the chair where Jackie had been sitting.

"Oh!" Jackie bent down and scooped up the loose pages. "Thank you. I would have walked out without it."

Quest nodded. "And if it is a tale which can be filmed by a young and inexperienced student crew for about two hundred thousand dollars, don't hesitate to synopsize it for me."

"I don't think this is movie material." Jackie smiled, patting the loose edges in place.

Taking Jackie's arm and leading her to the door, the famous film director chatted, "Oh, you'd be surprised—I've often used the word 'mortified'—to hear what the great gray minds of the film business, in their infinite wisdom, chose to option. The Bible, retyped and copyrighted, cookbooks, phrase books, tractor manuals . . ."

"No."

"But, yes," Quest insisted. "They actually got quite a delightful film out of that one. Beery and Marie Dressler, as I recall. I remember once in my early days as a producer without a project, I was scanning the acquisitions list and I noticed that they were contemplating buying a book whose French title loosely translated matched a novel they already owned. I checked, verified that this was indeed the case, and pointed it out to them, confident I would get a hearty pat on the back if not a small raise."

"Did you get either?" Jackie asked, strongly suspecting the answer.

"Of course not," Quest replied, opening the door. "They followed through and purchased the book anyway. 'Just to be sure' they said."

"Incredible," Jackie responded.

"Never actively discourage a moron from pursuing a dangerous course, Miss Walsh," the distinguished director advised as Jackie exited through the door. "It's like waving a red cape in front of a bull."

CHAPTER 3

Bill Curtis, the former mayor, spoke briefly, which was appreciated since no one had really wanted him to speak at all. He had not known the dead policeman. He had nothing to say about his passing. Indeed, when it came time for him to signal the combination Emerald Society and Masonic Honor Society band to play the funeral dirge, Mayor Curtis turned in the wrong direction and waved frantically to the honorary pallbearers.

The flag-draped coffin, dug up from where it had been first consigned, was placed in the hallowed ground of the Palmer Calvary Cemetery. The new plot had been paid for with contributions from Matthew Dugan's former comrades in arms. After the former mayor and the other handful of ersatz dignitaries had fled to their various dens of iniquity, Cosmo Gordon, holding on to the arm of the grief-stricken widow, said, "It's all over now, Xenia."

The hollow-eyed young woman, who had reluctantly left the deceased policeman shortly before his death, nodded. "All that separates us now, Cosmo, is six feet of . . . earth."

"Death be not proud, Xenia," the medical examiner intoned. "It comes for all of us. At least Matt knows now that his information helped us bring down the corruption ring that had this city by its throat."

"At what cost?" Xenia wailed, looking to her two morose children, now fatherless.

"At the usual cost, I'm afraid," Cosmo replied. He then noticed that the gravediggers were waiting to be tipped and that clearly Mrs. Dugan was in no condition to do it. Digging a couple of tens out of his wallet, Cosmo said, "Come, Mrs. Dugan, let's see if we can go somewhere and talk about where you go from here."

At the same time, Jackie whistled to herself a somewhat off-key version of "The Jitterbug." Could things be more wonderful? For the first time since she had returned to work at Rodgers Jackie actually felt like she was going to be able to make an impact somehow. Below her, as Jackie walked toward the parking lot, the sparkling Putnam reservoir shimmered and bubbled so beautifully it all but took her breath away.

It was just so good to have the water pure again.

Jackie tried not to dwell on the past—how it had been discovered the past September that Goodwillie Pharmaceuticals had been guilty of dumping pharmacological waste into the water system for nearly three years. The important thing was that the water was pure again.

All in all, Stuart Goodwillie had handled the situation well. He had immediately admitted the error, explaining that the valves and meters the Goodwillie plant had counted on to monitor waste levels had frozen shut when maintenance people had used too much metal polish.

Forthright and apologetic at his trial, without putting on so much as a single witness in his behalf (what good, after all, are character witnesses when you have been caught poisoning the water that babies drink from), Stuart Goodwillie had pled guilty and had thrown himself on the mercy of the court.

The people of Palmer appreciated Goodwillie's candor and decided that to put an old man in a federal penitentiary was cruel and wasteful. Instead, Stuart Goodwillie was charged with the task of cleaning up his own mess. The elderly pharmaceutical baron was happy to comply.

Unlike many American polluters, Goodwillie spent freely,

pouring tens of millions of dollars into the effort, and within six months the water was clean again. So clean, in fact, that bottled Palmer reservoir water soon became a best-selling item—creating new industry and new jobs.

No one had realized all those years how much the tainted water had affected everyday Palmer life. How it had touched so many lives leaving some people strange, lethargic, and confused.

In addition to the townspeople recovering their health and their ability to think and act reasonably, the people of Palmer now had something to look forward to—a large cash settlement from Goodwillie Industries.

At this very moment the new head of the city council, the courageous crusader Bonnie Greenspan, was hammering out the details of the final settlement. What would it mean to the citizens of Palmer? Would there be a one-time payment from the town of several thousand dollars that everyone could stick in their bank account? Or would the city council decide to take the lump sum and use it to pay off the deficit and then finance several public works? No one could tell as yet, and the pleasurable anticipation of knowing that something good was coming gave the whole town a Christmasy feel, even in the middle of the hottest summer on record.

While Jackie walked down quiet Chestnut Street she thought with pleasure that this was Thursday night. Poker night. The one night of the week that she and her mother and their friends, loosely referred to as the Gentle Lady Gambling Society, all met to gamble, gab, and gobble. What a fortunate thing, for if the events of the day were any indication, perhaps this was to be a lucky day for Jackie all the way around.

While his mother reflected on the fortunate turn of events that had rid her department of the secretarial lunatic, who was still guarding mimeograph paper although no one had used it for twenty years, Peter Walsh busily smashed pucks off the much-abused garbage cans in front of his house.

Jake, looking on approvingly, was the first to see it, and

a bark drew Peter's attention as well. While boy and dog watched, a strange silver and black Thunderbird, with a decal of a pirate flag with a dog's skull replacing the usual human one, cruised slowly down Sigourney Street, then made the turn and came up Isabella Lane right in front of the house. The driver of the car seemed to be searching for a specific address, and as Peter bent down to pick up his plastic liter of good Goodwillie Good Water, he wondered if whoever it was, was going to stop at his house.

CHAPTER 4

Frances Costello, Jackie's mother, was a picture of concentration as she pushed a little more mushroom cream cheese dip into the bugle-shaped cracker she held between her fingers. Frances liked to have things nice for her card parties, especially now that Jackie was coming regularly again.

Then, suddenly, Frances heard the elevator and rushed to the sink to rinse her hands. A moment later the doorbell rang and the still spry septuagenarian called out, "Use your keys, dear."

As Jackie struggled to open the locks her mother had installed since she had moved out so long ago, Frances located her dishtowel and pulled open the refrigerator door. Had she remembered to make room? Frances sighed with relief.

Jackie lugged the two bags of groceries she had brought for her mother into the large, high-ceilinged, exposed-brick kitchen and then surveyed the array of snacks that had already been laid out. "Just how many people are coming to the game tonight, Mother?"

Frances crossed over to her daughter and accepted a kiss on the cheek. "I just want things to be nice."

Jackie began to unpack the groceries. "Mother, did you remember Milly's coming with me?"

"Yes, dear," Frances responded. She then looked over Jackie's shoulder. "Oh, dear. You left the door open."

Jackie followed her gaze. "Sorry, my hands were full."

"That's why the Good Lord gave you legs and feet, dear," Frances yelled as she walked into the cluttered living room. "So you can kick a door closed when your arms are laden."

"And who would be the first to complain about shoeprints on her door?" Jackie yelled back as she folded the paper garbage bags neatly and put them in the canvas sack behind the kitchen door.

Frances returned to the kitchen. "Then use your hips, darling. They should be plenty strong for the purpose."

"Thank you, Mother." Jackie gave her progenitor a mock glare, then held up two six-packs of ginger ale. "What should I do with these?"

"There's space in the bottom, love," Frances replied. She then dragged a metal step stool over to the set of closets by the range.

"What about ice?" Jackie queried as she closed the refrigerator door. "You couldn't get a popsicle stick in that freezer."

"You shan't have to," Frances responded from on high. "I'm getting the punch bowl down now. The ice cubes can be plopped down right inside." Frances puffed and wiped her brow with effort. "You'd be doing me a favor, you know, if you took some things home."

Jackie opened the freezer door again and peered inside. "What can I take? Ice cream? Not after that remark about my hips."

Frances grunted as she tried again to tug the heavy silver bowl out of the smaller than advisable space it had been wedged into above her spiral cookbooks. "There's more than just sweets in there. There's stew, noodles. Take home some soda bread."

Jackie could be talked into that one. Groaning nearly as loudly as her mother, she pulled a frost-covered, foil-wrapped package of bread out of the overstuffed freezer compartment. "How is Mrs. Mulcahy?"

"She's coming tonight."

"Good."

"Got some good news. She doesn't have cataracts at all. It's pink eye. Oh, dear." Frances just caught herself as the old stepladder nearly overbalanced and tumbled her to the floor.

"Can I help you, Mother?" Jackie inquired.

"I wish you would," Frances responded with a sigh. Still a little shook up, she carefully descended the ladder and made her way back to her orange pillow-covered chair at the table.

Jackie scaled the ladder, snuck one foot on the range when her mother wasn't looking, and started to tug on the bowl.

"Watch you don't pull down the Betty Crocker books," Frances warned. "They're so old they'll be bits of paper all over the kitchen like a blizzard of yellow snow."

"I'll be careful," Jackie promised.

"I'll wipe off the stove after you go," Frances replied.

Jackie gave her mother a look, then fueled by aggravation, she yanked the bowl out of the closet. "Well," the young film instructor said, panting from the effort, as she placed the bowl on the table. "Speaking of good news, I had some today as well."

Frances gave her daughter a smile as she resumed putting her dip in her crackers. "What's that?"

"I talked to the new chairman—Ivor Quest. Place the name?"

Frances shook her head with pleasant incomprehension.

"Remember," Jackie said impatiently, "Ivor Quest was a film editor, then he directed all those big sweeping movies of the fifties and sixties."

"What sorts of movies could you make about sweeping?" Frances wondered.

"*Ryan's Girl,* Mother."

"That's not about sweeping."

"I know," Jackie said, her voice starting to get loud, "but that's one of the movies Ivor Quest made."

"Oh," Frances replied, now getting it. "I liked that one."

"So did I and now he's the new head of the Communication Studies department and—"

"Didn't like that Swedish woman, though."

"Yes, Mother."

Frances Costello drifted off on her own wavelength. "Can't think of her name. You know the one I mean."

"Mother—"

"Saint Joan, she was."

Jackie tried desperately to head her mother off. "Anyway, Mr. Quest gave me some wonderful—"

"And nuns. She played a couple of nuns! They all did that. You'd think once in all the history of the movies they could have found a story to tell where the Irish girl played a Protestant lay sister . . ."

"Mother, I am trying to tell you—"

"I'm not changing the subject," Frances protested indignantly. "It was you who brought up *Ryan's Girl*. All I'm saying was that Swedish girl who was good in certain things was not to my mind very convincing as a Derry lass."

"I agree with you, Mother," Jackie forced out. "Apparently everyone does. The movie was a terrible failure."

Frances nodded as if to say "What else?" then grabbed another bugle cracker to stuff with dip. "You see, she's a big strapping girl, which you can find in Derry, although that type is more common in the south. But that accent of hers. Ach. You know what my father said, if you can't speak the language you might as well go back to the silent films."

"There's no question, Mother, that Maureen O'Hara would have been a better choice, but to get back to—"

"Well, Maureen O'Hara." Frances Costello's face lit up at the mere mention of the saintly Hollywood actress's name. "Now you're not going to get an argument from me there. We don't know what she would have made of Golda Meir, of course, but if it's an Irish part you want someone to play, you could not do any better at all than Maureen O'Hara. There's very little doubt about that."

Jackie, knowing that it would be nearly impossible to get her mother back on track now, bent down and gave her a warm hug. "I'll see you later, Frances Cooley Costello."

Frances hugged her daughter's arms. "You're going home now to change? That's a girl. Put on that yellow dress your father bought for you."

This quickly straightened Jackie up. "Mother!"

"What's wrong with it? Don't tell me now that you can't fit . . . ?"

Jackie took a deep breath and explained patiently, "Daddy bought me that dress for college. I am now thirty-eight years old. If I have the dress at all, it's one of the rags I use for cleaning the Jeep."

"I . . ." Frances began with great dignity, "will be wearing the white chiffon outfit this evening that your father bought for me in 1946."

Jackie picked up her shoulder bag and prepared to escape. "I've dumped the ice in the bowl, Mother. Good-bye. Don't make the punch too strong."

"You don't have to drink it!" Frances's shrill voice chased Jackie into the next room. "You'd think with all that fuss we've been hearing about tainting the water you'd hesitate to suggest tampering with a two-hundred-year-old recipe for Costello Champagne Punch."

As Jackie made room for the foil-wrapped bread in her bag she saw the manuscript that she hadn't yet gotten a chance to look at. "Mother!"

"I thought you left," Frances snapped.

"In a minute. Do you remember one of Daddy's writer friends from TV?"

"Oh, sweet Jesus," Frances muttered. "One of his drinking buddies, d'ye mean? No disrespect to a dear man."

"No doubt," Jackie replied. "His name is Ralph Perrin. Does that ring a bell?"

Frances didn't respond as she scraped the last of her dip from the bowl with a spoon. "Oh, shame. Jackie, I broke this one, dear." Frances held up a crumbled bugle cracker.

"Would you like to take it with you?"

Jackie laughed. "Hide it in the middle. I'll have it when I come back."

At the same time, in Longacre Center, a shadowy figure used a key to open the door to Jackie's cubicle. Marcus Baghorn, the sleek, fast-talking advertising and marketing communications specialist, talking loudly on his speaker phone, looked up through his pebbled glass door and saw someone entering the cubicle across from his own. He put his phone caller on hold and walked over to the door. As he was about to close the door again he saw a familiar figure. "Oh, it's you," Marcus called out. "Thought I saw someone trying doors."

The person Marcus recognized gave a blank look as if to say "I know nothing about it," then disappeared around the bend of the corridor.

As Marcus went back to his desk he wondered to himself just what had happened. Rodgers University, for all its charms, certainly had a lot of strange, vaguely sinister characters running around unchecked.

CHAPTER 5

Jackie drove her Jeep a little faster through the streets than she had to, resisting the impulse to make her trip a little shorter by cutting across a few lawns.

When she arrived at home she was surprised to see a note pinned to the door. Peter was supposed to spend the night at his friend Isaac Cook's house. Jackie was always after her son to leave her a note and let her know what, if anything, was happening. It would be strange to find that apparently for once he had done just that—going to the trouble even of leaving an envelope stuck under the ornamental knocker on the front door. Jackie grabbed the envelope and punched her code into the button-lock that she had been forced to install since both she and her son were forever losing their keys.

The moment the door opened, Jake was at her feet. "Hello, big fellow!" She smiled, bending down to pat the lean, strong dog that she'd grown to love. "Glad to see me, eh?"

Jackie was a little surprised to find Jake so close to the front door. Normally he camped out under the kitchen table and either stood up or slowly padded over when she came in at night. Jackie put the matter out of her mind, however, distracted by the extreme stuffiness of the apartment. Peter was supposed to leave the air conditioner on low when he left, but, of course, he had neglected to do so.

Jackie flipped the envelope on the mail table, then walked over to turn on the air conditioner. Too humid days, like the one she had just lived through, played havoc with Jackie's allergies. Panting for a second like a dog to amuse her security guard, Jackie noticed for a second time that Jake was giving her an expectant look.

"What's the matter, Jake? What do you need? Water? Food?"

Jackie did not understand it, although she was not yet upset. Jake was usually remarkably good-natured. Having spent most of the first seven years of his life boarding at one Palmer police facility or another, the big dog had hardly been spoiled.

"Are you going to talk to me?"

Jake kept looking past Jackie to the door. Thinking perhaps he heard someone coming, Jackie walked back to the door and took a peek out. Nothing.

"Oh, well."

Jackie opened the drapes on the front window, then went into her bathroom and listened for a moment through the connecting wall between her home and the empty studio next door. "Maybe someone was showing the apartment, Jake," she explained.

Jake shrugged that off and looked again at the window.

Jackie shrugged too. She did not know what was happening, but figured if it was something, she would know soon enough.

The film professor lived with her son in an L-shaped two-family residence in what was called "the Water District." The former location of Palmer Regular Steel, a huge foundry and processing plant now closed, the Water District had experienced a bit of a comeback when some of the artists and students, unable to find suitable housing on campus, had reclaimed the industrial neighborhood for their own. Jackie had moved into the apartment thinking that it would be fun to live in Palmer's version of New York's Soho area. Unfortunately the remote neighborhood hadn't caught on as well as expected.

When Jackie had first moved in, the other part of the

duplex had been occupied by Freyda Persil and her son
Eric. Freyda was a very pleasant, very traditional Eastern
European-born woman with very little English, despite the
fact that she had lived in Palmer for fifteen years. Eric, a
bored, overweight child Peter's age, had played on the same
hockey team as he, and although he had irritated everybody
he came in contact with, not a day went by that Jackie did
not hear how the team had suffered since their leading high
sticker had moved away. Unfortunately, Mr. Persil, an iron
worker whom Jackie never did meet, finally found work in
Texas and sent for his family.

Since the Persils moved out, the studio had remained empty. Unfortunately the apartment was not really big enough
for a couple, and the trees on their side of the building
blocked off most of the light making the apartment quite
dark. Jackie had made it very clear to her landlord, a nice
Italian dentist who had retired to Florida after his invalid
mother died, that she did not want any part of showing
the apartment to potential renters. Subsequently, she had not
really noticed how often the agencies brought people by to
see it. She assumed that it did not happen too often, since
she had never seen or heard anything about it. But maybe
someone had come by earlier in the day and made noise in
the big wheelchair-access bathroom abutting her own.

"Could that be what has you so upset, big fella?" Jackie
called out. Shrugging away her lack of a better answer, Jackie
washed up, then joined Jake in the kitchen where he was now
placidly drinking from his dish. "Want to go out back for a
while, boy?"

Jake gave her a dripping smile and Jackie shucked off
her shoes. "Groan," she said. Although Jackie tried to wear
comfortable shoes, she just plain spent too much time on
her feet. She grabbed a can of diet chocolate soda out of
the refrigerator and followed Jake out into the backyard.

It was a beautiful night. Jackie collapsed into her lawn
chair and let the tension ease out of her body. This was
so nice. Jackie didn't get a chance to enjoy her tiny little

backyard plot of grass very often. It was usually dark when she got home, or if Peter was around he and his friends usually monopolized the space to play sports. It was times like this that she missed the huge lawns surrounding her former colonial home in the suburbs. Someday, Jackie decided, people would have both the convenience of living in a major city and the space now only associated with suburban dwellings like boring Kingswood. It also occurred to Jackie as she lay back, her feet on the living, vibrating cushion known as Jake's back, that even then people like her stuffy, barbecuing-in-the-backyard fiend, ex-husband Cooper would continue to live in dreary little enclaves with people just like himself.

"Enough of that," she said aloud. Jackie then pulled the rubber band-held manuscript onto her lap and decided to at least browse through it. She was really too tired to concentrate and in just a few moments she was going to have to take a shower and return to her mother's house for some cutthroat poker. However, if this Mr. Perrin really was her father's friend he deserved some consideration—and since he had already gone to the expense and trouble to fax the manuscript to her, it wouldn't be too surprising if he called her in the next few days. So, taking a sip of her diet chocolate, Jackie turned to the book's introduction.

She skimmed most of it since it seemed to concern only the wonderful and fascinating life Ralph Perrin had come to live before he decided to write this biography of Georgiana Bowman. Just before she got to the end of the introduction however, Jackie was caught by a little scene written in screenplay format. Jackie noted with some amusement that it seemed to be a parody of a scene from *Sunset Boulevard*, with Ralph standing in for William Holden, Georgiana Bowman standing in for Gloria Swanson, and some strapping Turhan Bey type character standing in for Eric Von Stroheim. Making a mental note to at least read that much when she returned home, Jackie labored to her feet and clicked her fingers for Jake to follow her.

Jackie was a little surprised when the big dog didn't immediately pad after her. "What's the matter, boy? It's cooler inside. Honest."

Jake just lay on his stomach, looking at the back of the empty studio that formed the right wall of the yard.

"There's no one there, Jake," Jackie assured him. "At least not that I know of."

Jake didn't react, so Jackie decided not to push it. "All right, listen. You can stay out here for a while. I've got to take a shower and change to go out. But you've got to come in later, all right? So you can watch the house while I'm gone. Okay?"

Jake finally turned his head to his mistress, batted his eyes at her, and then went back to watching the empty studio.

"Strange," Jackie said to herself. But then, it had been a strange day.

A long cool shower beat most of the fatigue from Jackie's weary body. By the time she emerged from her bedroom, comfortably dressed in a sand-colored cotton dress and espadrilles, even Jake seemed to have gotten over whatever was bothering him.

"Top of the morning to you, officer," Jackie cooed, rubbing the tight skin over the Alsatian's brow and jaws, making him grimace and drool. "How are you?" she asked, allowing the dog to rub his nose against the traces of after-bath lotion on her neck.

As Jackie looked around for her shoulder bag, Jake wandered over to the door of her bedroom. He then settled down to wipe the scent off his snout with his front paws, enjoying the process of breaking the perfume down into its component parts. This sort of activity gives dogs the same pleasant mental stimulation that humans get from crossword puzzles.

Jackie located her bag, keys, glasses, and the flask of mint iced tea made with good clean Goodwillie bottled water she had promised to bring. As she walked toward the door however, Jackie was surprised to find her dog entwining himself between her legs when she tried to get past him out the front door. This was a trick Jackie had hitherto only associated with cats.

"Do you want to go with me, Jake?" she asked.

The big dog's tongue immediately came out and his ears and tail wagged "Sure."

"All right." Jackie didn't usually think to bring Jake to her mother's because of Victor, but if it meant so much to the big dog, well, what the heck? "Let's go, then. I'm already late."

Jake hesitated, then walked back inside and put his chin on the telephone table.

"Jake," Jackie said impatiently. "I don't have to ask my mother's permission, honest. She likes you. Remember?"

The police dog waited very patiently in the same position until Jackie finally left the open front door and came over to the table. Wondering what it was her dog was up to exactly, Jackie reached for the receiver. She then saw the note that had been left on her door. The moment Jackie's hands closed on the note, Jake picked his head up off the table. "Is this what you wanted me to bring?"

Jake got up and trotted over to Jackie's shoulder bag by the front door.

"Should I read it now?"

Jake sat down by the bag and panted heavily.

"Jackie," the note began, "I'm in town for a day. Could we meet some time as we discussed on the phone?" The note was from Ralph Perrin, apparently. It went on to tell her where he was staying and that he was anxious to talk with her.

Jackie gave Jake a look. The big dog woofed, apparently reminding her that she did not have time to think about this.

Jackie made a face and then picked up the phone. She push-buttoned the number of Perrin's hotel quickly and after a number of rings spoke to the operator. "Mr. Perrin, please . . . Oh, he's out? Will you please tell him

that Jackie Walsh called and left a message that I can
meet him briefly tomorrow morning. At ten o'clock. At
the Longacre Center for Communications Studies on the
Rodgers University campus. Tell him to ask for the Faculty Lounge and he doesn't have to return my call to
confirm. I expect to be out most of the evening and
will return quite late. All right? Yes, he has my number.
Thank you."

Jackie then turned to Jake. "Satisfied?"

Jake nodded and then trotted out the door with the shoulder
bag in his teeth.

Jackie looked after him a moment and wondered, not for
the first time, whether maybe she would not have been hap-
pier with a nice little goldfish.

Death, illness, autumn marriages, and the inevitable spe-
cies urge to migrate south to Florida had thinned the ranks
of Frances Costello's old round table. As it was, when Jackie
and her friend Milly arrived at the Costello apartment shortly after seven o'clock, they almost doubled the number of
guests.

"Mother!" Jackie said at once.

"Jacqueline Shannon." Frances liked to use both of Jackie's
names. "You remember Maggie Mulcahy?"

Jackie nodded her head at her mother's oldest friend in
the world, a sweet, dark-haired, retired telephone operator
with swollen puffy pink eyes who had known Frances since
Catholic school.

"It's good to see you, Jackie," Maggie said, reaching out
her hand somewhat blindly. "Although I really can't see
anything unless it's right in front of my nose." Then, as if
to prove the point, Maggie dropped a mini-cheesenut ball
off the Ritz cracker she was holding while the other women
watched it roll under the couch.

"I'll vacuum that later," Frances said, smiling. "Who else?
Well, you remember Jean Scott? She is in the bathroom at
present but should soon rejoin us. And this is Maggie's friend

who was nice enough to drive her here tonight, whose name I'm afraid I've forgotten."

A tall woman with red curly hair resembling somewhat a full-grown Little Orphan Annie with pupils stuck out her hand. "Hanna Longmuir."

Jackie took her hand. "Jackie Walsh. And this is my friend from the college, Milly Brooks."

"Hi, guys!" Milly said brightly.

Frances, thinking to bail herself out for forgetting Ms. Longmuir's name, piped up, "Hanna has a fascinating job . . ." Frances then came up short as that too slipped away from her. "But I'll be darned if I can remember what it was. Something to do with earth, as I recall."

Hanna, smiling as if this sort of thing happened to her every day of the week, obligingly supplied the answer, "I sell it, actually. I work for a national real estate agency. As a commission salesperson."

"FutureLand?" Milly said brightly.

"Why, yes. Did you recognize . . . ?"

"It was just a guess," Milly admitted, shucking off her light jacket and digging into the hors d'oeuvres. "All those commercials on TV."

"Yes," Hanna responded warily, not sure if she was being complimented or put down. "FutureLand Industries believes in keeping a high nationwide profile."

"Love those green blazers." Milly smiled again. "Very horsey. I'm always trying to get John to wear something like that. Without the patch, of course." Leaving Hanna more confused than ever, Milly's fingers unerringly moved to the one broken bugle cracker on the plate. "Oops, look, Frances."

Mrs. Costello glared at her daughter as she was pulled by her into the kitchen. "Didn't I tell you to take the broken cracker with you?" she asked.

"Never mind that, Mother," Jackie responded, giving the beautifully dressed Irish lady a first-class scowl. "What did I . . . ?"

"I know." Frances tried to make placating gestures, but they were to no avail.

"*Six* poker players!"

"I know."

"You promised, Mother," Jackie exploded. "Five to a table. Five players or ten players. In a pinch eight players for two tables of four. We've been doing this for years now, and if it's one thing we all agree on, is that six people to a table doesn't work at all."

"Take a knife from the table and cut your poor old mother's throat with it," Frances instructed.

"Mother."

"Please, Jackie," Frances sighed. "You know I try desperately to do things the way you like. But I haven't had a game in so long people have gotten out of the habit of Thursdays."

"Well, if you told me you expected just three people I would have come myself without Milly."

"Now, Jacqueline, don't be like that. It's not Maggie's fault that she got pink eye and couldn't drive herself. And I don't know this Hetty woman . . ."

"Hanna."

"But if she spends all of her day with those horrible real estate people you see doing commercials on TV then I'm sure she's just about desperate to while away an evening with some decent people."

Jackie sighed deeply. There went her perfect day. "All right, mother. But please—only five at the table at any one time. The sixth will have to sit out."

"I'm a slave to your wishes, dear," Frances lied as she poured herself a healthy snifter of champagne punch. "Care for a snort?"

"Not yet," Jackie replied. "Where's Victor?"

"At Bara Day's house. I thought with all the strangers here, we'd spare the poor fellow any upset."

Jackie raised an eyebrow. A fourteen-foot python, Victor was unlikely to be upset by anything short of a nuclear weapon. "Is it all right if I bring Jake in, then?"

"Of course. Where is he? You didn't lock the poor thing in that truck of yours, did you?"

"It's a Jeep, mother. And no, Jake's in the courtyard. I'll go get him."

The Strang Arms Apartment Complex had been a fixture on the north side of Palmer since World War I. The buildings had been slightly modified over the years. Jackie's parents had moved into the complex shortly after she was born and had kept the apartment, even in the years when Pete Costello had spent most of his time in Hollywood. The courtyard was a big open plaza with benches and strips of grass. The flower beds were not very well kept up and the trees were propped up by so many boards and chains and braces that they might have well been artificial, but the area was still a cool place to sit on a warm summer evening, and a delight for visiting canines 365 days a year.

"Hello, Jake!" Jackie called out when she entered through the low archway. "Where are you?"

Jake bounded over happily. The old investigator had been doing a little sleuthing around some garbage bins in the back archway near the laundry room.

"Having a good time?"

The dog woofed in the affirmative and gave a nod as if indicating for her to follow him to a particularly revealing tree stump.

"I can't right now, Jake. I have to go back upstairs. You okay down here?"

The big dog wagged his tail.

"All right." Jackie bent down and fed Jake some corned beef strips she had filched from the banquet table. "Why don't you stay down here and poke around for a while, and I'll come back down and collect you on my next break? Okay?"

Jake nodded solemnly, and with a lick of his lips to capture any leftover salt particles, he returned to his investigations.

Jackie went back upstairs.

By the time Jackie got back to the apartment, Frances was ready for a break so her daughter slid easily into her mother's chair.

"The game is seven-card stud," Jackie announced. "Deuces wild low—one-eyed jacks wild high—and, of course, the the Suicide king can change suits. Ten cents to ante, five cents to raise, three bumps per round. Any questions?" Jackie riffled the deck, making the playing cards obediently mountain high and valley low. Then as the other ladies looked on amazedly, Jackie flicked the cards from one hand to the other as if playing a concertina before slapping the deck on the table to her left for Hanna to cut.

"Is this your first time on the riverboat, miss?" Hanna joked.

Jackie waited for the laughs to subside, then started dealing the cards.

Jackie's entrance into the game cooled the gossip for a few moments as the players concentrated. After about twenty minutes of spirited play, however, the group took a break and when Hanna volunteered to accompany Jackie down to the courtyard to check on Jake, the two women got a chance to talk for a few moments.

"So, are you originally from this area?" Jackie asked as they emerged into the courtyard.

"No," Hanna replied, lighting up a cigarette. "I'm from California."

Jackie nodded and did a few unkinking exercises as they walked toward where she had last seen Jake. "Tired of the smog?"

"Actually," Hanna replied, sipping from the cup of strong black coffee she had brought down with her, "I was asked to come here by the main office. They see Palmer as a hot new territory and they're bringing in myself and several other successful salespeople from different parts of the country to establish a professional office here."

"Really?" Jackie forgot about looking for her dog for a moment and turned to give the real estate saleswoman her full attention. "Why is Palmer so hot all of a sudden? Just because Goodwillie Pharmaceuticals cleaned up the water?"

Hanna nodded. "In a way. More of it has to do with the anticipated settlements."

"I don't understand."

"Really? I should think this is all common knowledge here. Your city administration is going to be offering interest-free loans to apartment dwellers or home owners moving into certain districts in town—the South Side, Robin Hill, the Water District . . ."

"The Water District? . . ." Jackie was amazed to hear all of this. "That's where I live."

Hanna shrugged. "Well, expect to have all kinds of new neighbors. The word is City Hall is going to pour a great deal of the Goodwillie settlement money into your neighborhood. They are trying to rent the empty apartments, sell the empty homes, and turn the empty buildings into condominiums. The next step after that, or so we hear, is that they'll turn the old foundry into a mall and recreation area."

"Really?"

"Oh, yes," Hanna replied glibly. "And there are similar plans for the South Side and Robin Hill. Your city could be very, very popular in just a few years."

Jackie was reflecting on that point when a window opened on the corridor and a familiar Irish-accented voice called down. "Ladies! Back to the table, please. We said we'd make this an early evening. Let's not spend it all just socializing, shall we?"

"Coming!" Jackie yelled up. She then turned to Hanna. "Why don't you tell them I'll sit out for a while? I still have to corral this mutt of mine."

Hanna nodded and said in parting, "Wouldn't you just love to be able to turn this place into condos?"

Jackie looked around her. Most of the apartments in the old building had windows that faced the courtyard. When Jackie

was a little girl she remembered always seeing these windows
open. Air conditioners were a luxury item then. The air was
clean enough then that windowboxes and canary cages were
regular fixtures. Clotheslines had crisscrossed the airspace
and almost every sill was cushioned with a pillow so that
neighbors could hang out and chat. Twenty years ago a dark
window would have meant that the families were out for
the evening—dancing, visiting, bowling, playing miniature
golf, or going to the movies. No more. Now, almost every
window had its drapes or blinds closed. Behind the more
translucent drapes Jackie saw the blue electric blur of a
television screen. Twenty years ago, Jackie reminisced, the
courtyard could have passed for the one in *Rear Window*.
Today the courtyard after dark was simply a place for dogs
to go to the bathroom.

"Hello, Jake," Jackie greeted her dog as he suddenly
materialized at her side. "Having fun?"

The dog shrugged and then sat down to scratch behind
his neck.

"I was just talking to someone who thought this whole
building should be turned into condos and that this courtyard
should be turned into a restaurant."

Jake had no reaction.

"They don't understand that people in Palmer don't buy
real estate to impress their neighbors. They buy homes so
they have somewhere to live for the rest of their lives."

Jake nodded his wise old head and got back onto his
feet.

Jackie shivered a little and then reached down to pat her
faithful companion. "Let's go back up, Jake."

When she sat back down, giving Maggie Mulcahy another
chance to sprawl out on the couch with a wet cloth over her
swollen eyes, Jackie more or less mechanically played the
next few hands. By this time, the game had come down
basically to Frances and Hanna, with Jackie still in it only
by virtue of the fact that she had sat out so many hands.

When Jackie lost her third straight hand without putting up much of a fight, Jake decided he would get involved.

Fortunately at that moment they were playing a game of straight draw poker, a game his mistress had taught him a great deal about. Ducking under the table, Jake came up between Jackie's legs and immediately demanded to see her hand. Without really thinking about it, Jackie obliged. After studying her cards for a long moment, Jake disappeared only to do the same with each of the other ladies in turn until he knew the contents of each player's hand. Jackie, the only one who was able to get even the slightest glimmer that Jake was not looking for affection or food, but actually trying to help, sat up straight in her chair and kept a careful eye on her dog during the playing of the next hand.

"I'll open," Frances announced, after everyone had gotten a chance to study their cards. She pushed a nickel's worth of chips into the center of the table and then looked over to Jake. The dog, seemingly ignoring the goings-on at the table, was playing with a bowl of chips he had managed to overturn onto the carpet. When Jake stuck his head into the bowl so as to wear it as a crown, Jackie softly said to herself, "Kings, eh?"

The others matched Frances's bet and threw in their discards so that they could get more cards. Jackie had a decision to make. She had one ace and three of her other cards were clubs. If no one at the table had aces, then the pair would probably be easier to draw than two clubs. In addition, in a game of draw poker without wild cards, two aces could well be a winning hand. On the other hand, if there were aces out or if anyone else had a pair, then Jackie was best advised to try to make the flush.

"Jake, what are you doing?" Jackie said. "Excuse me." She got up, retrieved the bowl, and put it back on the table. "How many aces are out, partner?" she whispered.

Jake got up and slowly bent a paw in the direction of Jean Scott.

The reviewer, not knowing what was going on, laughed. "Oh, is he a pointer too?"

"No," Jackie joked back. "He knows that pointing isn't polite." Jackie then hugged the big dog to her. "And he's a good dog, aren't you, Jake?" As the big dog licked his mistress's face, she whispered, "What about pairs?"

Jake pulled loose and went over and brushed Hanna's chair. She looked down, then turned back to her hand, deciding on the cards she wanted to discard.

Jackie looked at Jake who had turned to face her. She raised her eyebrows. The dog's tail brushed against Hanna's chair, once, twice, three, four times.

"Pair of fours," Jackie mumbled to herself. "Okay."

"Sit down, Jacqueline Shannon," Frances instructed. "This is the last hand of the night and you're making us nervous."

"Sorry," Jackie said, moving back over to the table. She then quickly seated herself and threw in her ace and seven. She would go for the flush.

When the players received their new cards, Jake once again made the rounds.

"Does he have to go out or something?" Frances asked as Jake studied her hand, then laid back down.

"I think so," Jackie said. "We'll light out of here as soon as this hand's finished."

"Could I beg a ride from you, Jackie?" Jean asked. "I hate to wait for the bus this late."

"Of course," Jackie responded automatically. She was watching Jake.

"Well, I guess since I opened, I might as well start the betting," Frances announced. "Ten cents."

Jake, apparently needing a good stretch, rolled over on his back, then held up first his front paws, then his back paws.

Two pairs, Jackie thought to herself. So far so good—for she had gotten the flush.

Jackie pushed twenty cents into the middle of the table. "I'll see you, Mother, and raise you ten cents."

Jean was next. "I'll see your twenty cents and raise you ten."

Jackie looked at Jake. He rolled over dead. She was bluffing.

Hanna's turn now. "I'll see your thirty cents . . ."

Jake turned around and nipped at something on his rear end.

Hanna had gotten her ace.

Jake barked twice.

Two aces. "Just a minute, dear," Jackie said pleasantly.

"And I'll raise ten cents," Hanna announced.

This would normally be the last bet but since this was the last hand, another round was permitted.

Frances looked at her cards again, Jake peeked again to make sure he remembered them correctly, and then Jackie's mother announced, "Well, let's see. I've got my lucky orange cushion on my seat, so I'm going to go for broke. How much is it to me to call?"

"Thirty cents, Mother," Jackie said quickly.

"Look at her. The fruit of my womb and she can't wait to strip me of my laundry money. All right. How sharper than a serpent's tooth and all."

"Are you talking about that snake of yours again?" Maggie called out from the front room.

Ignoring her fuzzy-eyed friend, Frances licked a thumb and then started pushing coins into the middle of the table. "I see your thirty cents and raise you twenty cents."

Jackie jumped in. "I see your forty cents and raise you ten."

Jean Scott, giving Jake a suspicious look, declared, "This is too rich for my blood," and threw in her cards.

Hanna, also aware that something was up, pushed in thirty cents. "I call."

Jackie laid down her cards with a flourish. "Read them and weep," she said.

And Jake obliged with a mournful howl.

• • •

Later, driving Jean Scott home, Jackie felt moved to comment, "You know, Miss Scott, I was just thinking about you today."

"Well," Jackie's passenger replied, "if you know me well enough to daydream about me, you know me well enough to call me Jean. What were you thinking about? How you and your dog could rook a poor, helpless widow?"

"No." Jackie laughed. "Nothing like that."

"I must say," Jean continued in her same dryly humorous tone. "He does seem to have made a tremendous recovery from his Colt .45 magnum wound."

The two women shared a hearty laugh. During those dread tainted water days, someone had spread a rumor that Jake had been shot in the leg with a gun the size of a small cannon. What had actually happened, of course, was that the poor dog had stepped on a piece of glass from a shattered magnum of champagne.

"When is your paper going to print a retraction?" Jackie joked back.

"If that's what you're waiting for, you're going to have to wait a long time," Jean averred. "I swear, I don't know what historians are going to make of the last six months of *Herald*s we put out. I guess we hope they'll think that the journalists of Palmer just pulled off the longest April Fool's joke in history."

"Let's hope so," Jackie replied with a smile. "What about you? Are you going to go back and reread all those books you reviewed to see if you still believe what you wrote?"

"Oh, dear," Jean groaned. "Don't even joke of such a thing. I have such a backlog now, I don't know when I'll see the top of my desk again. It's terrible. Now I'm committed to reading morning, noon, and night until Christmas just to catch up."

"Just don't tie up your Thursday nights."

"Well, of course poker night remains sacrosanct. I told my editor long ago," Jean related, "I wouldn't skip my Thursday night card game for a chance to read a long-lost Jane Austen manuscript."

"Really?" Jackie was impressed. There was no more devoted Jane Austen fan in the universe than the intelligent, white-haired Jean Scott.

"Of course not, darling. I'm drunkenly resorting to hyperbole." Jean paused for a moment, then tentatively started, "Jackie . . ."

"Yes?"

"You'll think this awfully nosy of me, dear. But I'm afraid I must ask. I noticed before we left, when I passed by your bag, that you had a manuscript tucked inside. Don't tell me you're holding up the great Costello tradition and are attempting a novel?"

"Oh, no." Jackie laughed. "Not yet, anyway, as Dad used to say. It's a book that was sent to me from an old friend of Pop's. He wants me to pass it along to someone at the University Press."

Jean relaxed in her seat. "Oh, dear. Not one of those dreary kiss and tell autobiographies, I hope."

"I hope not too," Jackie replied honestly. "First of all the U wouldn't publish anything that superficial. And second of all, I'd really like to read a good book on Georgiana Bowman and see it on the stands."

"Georgiana Bowman." Jean took a moment to place the name. "Wasn't she a director or something, in silent films?"

"A little after that, but yes, she's one of the great movie pioneers."

"And who is this intrepid archaeologist who has managed to unearth enough data on Cavewoman Georgiana to make up a slim volume? Some UCLA professor?"

"A writer named Ralph Perrin," Jackie answered.

"Ralph Perrin?!"

Jackie turned onto Jean Scott's street on Robin Hill. "Do you know him?"

"Like I know John Dillinger. Dear, Ralph Perrin is to plagiarism as Willie Sutton is to bank robbery."

"Uh-oh."

As the Jeep pulled up in front of Jean Scott's small gray, tree-shrouded residence, the elderly book reviewer grabbed Jackie's arm. "Do yourself a favor, dear. Before you go out on a limb for this man, come by sometime. I'll take a break from my reading and tell you a little off-the-record information about your father's good friend, Ralph."

With a sinking feeling and a sense that her wonderful day had suddenly ended, Jackie watched Jean walk up the leaf-strewn walk to her house, enter, and slowly close the door.

CHAPTER 6

The first thing in the morning, Jackie was outside in her warm-up suit, the tense, powerful Jake at her side. As they walked along Faculty Lane past the austere late nineteenth-century row houses where the deans of the college and most senior faculty members lived, Jackie thought of the man she was scheduled to meet that day.

Sometime in the next few days Jackie would go by Jean Scott's and pick up her file on Ralph Perrin. Even before she did such a thing, Jackie could tell that something was wrong with the whole affair.

Jackie had been too tired to do more than glance through the manuscript when she had returned home after the poker game. Even a cursory look, however, had put her off the book. First of all, the biography didn't seem to be very well written. Large sections were simply articles or interviews with Georgiana Bowman published in the thirties or forties in now-defunct magazines. The articles were scrupulously credited to their original authors and presumably Ralph had gotten whatever permission was necessary to reprint them, but this hardly constituted a biography.

Perrin's own writing in the book—the very long, very strange preface that seemed to consist entirely of introductory comments before each of the excerpts, a paragraph or two after each article summing up what the reader had just read, and handwritten marginalia throughout the reprinted sections—was the weirdest touch of all. Much of it was tasteless, at times going over into downright libel. A lot of the comments seemed to indicate that he, Perrin, did not agree with what was being said by the author. It was true that some of the writers included in the book, particularly in the articles reprinted from the plethora of fan magazines that flourished in the early forties, had a rather cloying writing style, but it simply made one wonder why, if Perrin had disliked their writing so much, he had chosen to reprint their articles in his book?

The places where Perrin's comments seemed to indicate that he flatly disagreed with what was being written were equally mystifying. Since Perrin never cited sources in his comments section, one could not tell why he felt the way he did, and again one had to wonder why he included stories in his book that he knew to be untrue.

What were these comments all about? Jackie wondered. Did he intend for them to appear in the margins exactly as they were placed in her manuscript? Jackie was at a loss to conclude whether these comments were meant to be part of the book or whether they were just bitter jokes or quips to amuse her or the intended publisher.

In short, Ralph Perrin seemed ambivalent about everything in the book—the subject of the book, the veracity of the authors he had selected to be included, and most of all about whether or not he wanted to write a biography of the woman he had chosen to write about.

All of this left Jackie equally ambivalent. She still felt a book on Georgiana Bowman should be written and that this book, for all its flaws, did give a fairly good overview of the pioneer director's career. But it seemed entirely likely that Perrin was going to have to rewrite sections of the book. He was going to have to lose at least some of the quips at the other authors' expense. Further, Perrin was going to have to tighten up his introduction and the end section, which seemed at first to sum up Georgiana Bowman's career, but which in fact ended so abruptly it was difficult to tell whether that coda was unfinished or this was simply another stylistic choice that didn't work.

As Jackie walked through the metal gates of the college, she worried about what she was going to say to the man. How would he react to her suggestions for massive rewrites? Would he expect her to hold his hand during the rewrites or keep reading subsequent drafts? This was something that Jackie really dreaded. She disliked doing this even for her favorite, most promising students; she really didn't want to get roped into doing this for a man who was for all intents and purposes a perfect stranger.

With all these thoughts in mind, Jackie entered the Rodgers Field House with Jake at her heels.

The Rodgers jocks were already out in force, stretching and running laps. Jackie nodded to a few who seemed familiar and tried to look pleasant as an enormous basketball player, just dripping sweat, stopped to pet a stoic Jake who clearly didn't like the attention. Then, telling the big dog to wait by a glass-enclosed fire hose, Jackie went inside the women's locker room.

Things were quiet. Only a few people other than Jackie were changing and they, like her, were still quietly half asleep. This locker room, unlike the men's locker room, was free of sexy posters. The only notices were those neatly tacked to the bulletin board and they referred mostly to health matters. When Jackie went to her own locker in the small faculty section, she noted with approval that for once the garbage cans had been emptied, the rubber runners had been mopped, and, miracle of miracles, even the little rugs by the water fountains had been vacuumed.

Jackie opened her combination lock, peeled off her sweat suit, and hung it on the one hook. Feeling creaky and old, Jackie put on her clogs and swimming cap. She then hung her goggles around her neck, grabbed the oversize fluffy towel that all swimmers prefer but that no public pool ever provides, and said softly to herself, "I am going to be lucky to swim half a mile today." Rinsing off under one of the

showers, Jackie then walked out to the pool area. She blinked
in the strong sunlight coming from the translucent ceiling,
adjusted her goggles, shivered briefly, then ran out onto the
low board and dived.

It was so nice to be swimming again.

Kicking furiously, Jackie traversed most of her lane underwater, then came up for a breath. Whew. Maybe she was
going to be able to do this after all. Swimming to the end,
Jackie executed a kick that was not half bad and then swam
vigorously to the other end.

After one of her quickest half miles in recent memory,
Jackie pulled herself out, a little wobbly-legged but breathing
all right, and climbed the ladder to the high board. Forcing
herself to concentrate over the noise of what she presumed
to be the arriving swim team, Jackie executed a perfect dive
into the water. When she came up, nearly at the other end of
the pool, she saw that she was no longer alone. There, on the
edge of the pool, standing by her towel and flip flops was a
policeman, one Lieutenant McGowan.

"Michael," she sputtered. "What are you doing here?"

"Sorry to bother you, Jackie," the tall plainclothes policeman replied. "But may I have a word with you?"

Normally Jackie would have been embarrassed to be seen
in public in only a bathing suit—especially since Michael
was as close as anyone to being her "love interest"—but as
she pulled herself up out of the pool, she could tell from the
dark Irishman's countenance that this was not a social call.

"What is it, Michael? What's wrong? Is is Peter? Or my
mother?"

McGowan shook his head impatiently as he handed Jackie
her towel. "What can you tell me about Ralph Perrin? Is it
true you have an appointment to see him today?"

Jackie nodded and glanced up at the clock in the water
polo scoreboard. "Yes. Not for another hour or so."

McGowan's eyes held Jackie's without affection. "He's
not going to make that appointment, Jackie. At seven o'clock
this morning Pacific time the Los Angeles police department

dragged Ralph Perrin out of the swimming pool of his hotel. He'd been dead for several hours."

Jackie felt her skin contract and not just because she was cold. "A heart attack or . . . ?"

"I'm here in my capacity as a homicide detective, Jackie. May I have a few words alone with you to discuss this matter?"

Jackie was still shivering as she sat in the interrogation room at the Palmer Central Police Precinct. Jake, no stranger to the building, nuzzled her leg and forced his snout into her hand. Jackie's hand automatically slipped over the big head and scratched her friend behind his ears. This simple action relaxed her and Jackie found herself regaining control.

"You're a good dog, Jake," she said finally.

Jackie then sat up straight as she heard the heavy metal door open.

"Sorry to take so long," McGowan apologized. "I had to talk to the captain." The homicide lieutenant put a donut shop giveaway plastic mug in front of Jackie. She grabbed it gratefully and took a long swallow of the delicious fresh-roasted coffee characteristic of most police stations, who do, after all, have access to the most wonderful coffee makers in the world, which they borrow from their property rooms until the burglary victims get around to reclaiming them.

"Before we go on record, Jackie," McGowan started, pointing to a cassette recorder between them, "I want to explain something."

Jackie pursed her lips and gave the lieutenant her full attention.

"I'm sorry I had to bring you down here like this. I'm just following orders."

"Heil Hitler," Jackie mumbled.

"Please. We're not sure whether or not Mr. Perrin was actually murdered. But he died under very mysterious circumstances and the Los Angeles police department wants to be very thorough in finding out just what happened."

"I understand," Jackie replied coldly.

"Do you?"

"I understand you have a job to do," Jackie snapped. "So do I. Why don't you ask me what you want? I have an eleven o'clock class to teach."

"I know." McGowan started to say something else, then choked it off. "At any time during this interrogation you may refuse to answer questions or request an attorney to be present."

"I know," Jackie replied in the same tone of voice.

McGowan sighed and turned on the tape recorder. "We resume questioning Ms. Jacqueline Walsh, at 9:57 A.M. Ms. Walsh, we've brought you here because your telephone number was the last number Mr. Perrin called, apparently, before he died. Could you tell us how you came to know the deceased?"

"Mr. Perrin?"

"Yes." McGowan gave Jackie a small smile, remembering that this was not the first time that they had discussed the life of the recently deceased.

"I didn't."

"Just a minute," a surprised McGowan blurted out. "Are you saying you don't know Ralph Perrin at all?"

"That's exactly what I'm saying," Jackie maintained firmly. "I have no recollection of ever having met the man you say they found in some Hollywood swimming pool. May I go now?"

"Not just yet . . . Ms. Walsh. Let's not confuse things here. You told me on the record earlier this morning that you did have an appointment to meet with a Mr. Ralph Perrin today at ten o'clock. Now are you changing that part of your statement?"

"No. You asked me if I knew him. As far as I know, I never met him."

"But you did speak to him?"

"Several days ago I spoke to a man who said he was Ralph Perrin. I don't know that he was."

"And he made an appointment with you then to meet today?"

"No."

"No . . . All right, then." McGowan made an attempt to stay calm. He knew Jackie was making it hard for him because she resented the fact that he had dragged her down here to the police station to be questioned. What she didn't know, apparently, was that with the ongoing corruption investigation going on in the Palmer police department, he really didn't have any choice. "How is your coffee, incidentally?"

Jackie had her back up and wasn't giving an inch. "I have a coffee maker in my own office, Lieutenant."

"I know," McGowan said softly.

"Are there any more questions for me?"

"What was the conversation about?"

"He introduced himself as a friend of my father's. He seemed to know my dad, he seemed to know me. Mr. Perrin basically wanted to send me a manuscript for a book he said he'd written on a female motion picture director in the thirties. He wanted me to recommend it to the University Publishing Press. I agreed to take a look at it and see what I could do."

McGowan nodded and made a note on his pad. "This was on Wednesday night?"

Jackie nodded and, without thinking, drank some more of the coffee.

"And he also set up a meeting with you for today?"

"No."

McGowan looked up from his notes.

"He mentioned," Jackie continued, "that we might get together and reminisce about my father. I agreed but didn't commit to any specific meeting. At the time I had no idea he was planning to come to Palmer himself in a couple of days."

McGowan nodded, taking her point. "Isn't it odd he didn't mention his upcoming trip to you?"

"I didn't know Mr. Perrin at all," Jackie repeated. "I have no idea what was odd for him and what wasn't."

"So when was it that he made arrangements with you to meet today?"

"I found an envelope taped to my door when I came home yesterday," Jackie related. "There was a note inside that purported to come from Ralph Perrin saying he was in town for another matter and asking if we could meet. He said he was at the Merrifield. I called there and left a message with the operator for him to meet me in the Faculty Lounge this morning."

McGowan straightened up in his chair and gave Jackie a hard look. "You're saying that a man left you a note here in Palmer just hours before he was found murdered in Los Angeles?"

"I'm not saying anything of the kind, Lieutenant. I said the note purported to come from Ralph Perrin. I keep telling you, I didn't know the man. I didn't know his handwriting. I didn't know his travel plans and I certainly didn't know that he was going to die in a swimming pool in Los Angeles instead of meeting with me today."

McGowan let Jackie calm herself, then resumed evenly, "I understand all of that, Ms. Walsh. I repeat, you are not under suspicion for anything. We are simply trying to untangle what has happened here. If we can establish that Mr. Perrin never set a foot in Palmer, then we can wash our hands of this entire investigation and go back to solving our own crimes."

"It's not quite that easy, Lieutenant," Jackie remarked, getting to her feet. "Somebody put a note on my door. If it wasn't him and if he was murdered, then the person who left me that note may have been the person who killed him."

CHAPTER 7

Normally Jackie would have canceled her eleven o'clock and let Suki take the class or show a movie. Today, however, she decided to go ahead and give the lecture. She was weary of canceling classes to solve crimes. Jackie had no real ambitions to do this sort of thing and was getting tired, frankly, of always being mixed up in mysterious killings. Also this was an important lecture, and with Ivor Quest on campus, Jackie was determined to show him that she was worthy of the support and help he had promised her.

"Film . . ." Jackie began, surveying the fairly large class sitting comfortably in their seats in the small, first-floor auditorium of the Longacre Communications Center the Film department used to screen its movies. "There is something chemical about the medium that affects us in ways that vinyl or video or laser disk impregnation hasn't been able to duplicate. A movie or film becomes not only a piece of history, but a work of art—the same way an oil painting achieves that status, when a charcoal drawing or a tapestry or rendering with chalk or ink does not. Why? Do we know? Can we say? In our last session you watched scenes from several movies that never made it into the final print. Those scenes, excised for various reasons from the final versions of the movies they were intended for, have no real status now. They're like pieces of canvas cropped from cut-down paintings or studio versions of songs that were never released

and yet they have the power to entertain. You may not have
been in your most relaxed frame of mind as you watched that
reel of scenes since you were, after all, taking a quiz . . ."

Jackie paused for chuckles and a few good-natured boos.
"But those scenes, reedited and perhaps linked together with
narration provided by someone like Pete Smith or Larry King
or John Forsythe, could be easily turned into a movie that
millions of people would pay good money to see. Why?
Because well-made movies, even pieces of well-made movies, have the power to draw you in and keep you interested no
matter who you are or how relevant the characters or the story
being depicted on the screen are to your understanding.

"Case in point. Roll the first clip, please. This is a scene
from *The Good Earth*. We are instantly caught up in this
scene, in this little drama of two farmers who have worked
so hard but are about to have their crop destroyed by locusts.
Look at them. We know this isn't real life, this is a scene
from a book written by a woman, then very popular, who
doesn't have a single book in our university bookstore. What
did the producer of this film know about Chinese farmers?
Nothing. He produced the film because his studio assigned
him to do it. Why did they buy it? Because the book was
a best-seller. Audiences of the thirties loved this movie.
It was a tremendous hit. Wildly successful although the
least sophisticated moviegoer knew that these people weren't
farmers; they were hammy American actors. They knew that
it had not been filmed in China around the turn of the century.
They knew it had just been shot in an almond grove near
Los Angeles, California, because they read about it daily
in the entertainment section of their newspapers. We know
today, whether or not they did, that the storm was a bunch of
giant wind machines and that the locusts were bits of twisted
brown paper and a plastic bag of coffee grounds shook in
front of the camera lens. Yet, we respond to it even though
no single part of it is true. Now roll the video."

The students' heads switched to a different screen.

"What we're seeing now is true. Last year in Los Angeles,

California, a black man and his passengers were stopped by policemen, ordered out of their car, and the driver was beaten. The policemen were real. The victim was real. The violence was real, not special effects. The location was real. The video was shot in real time. The short-term impact on us was strong, hard. This video caused riots in a dozen American cities. And yet it didn't have the capacity to convince a jury that what happened here was serious enough to convict three men of a crime. It seems horrible, terrible, like our world is some miserable hell, yet the same thing happened in the sixties."

Jackie gave a nod to Suki, her assistant, and the lights were soon restored.

"I was a student in the first Communications class course offered at this university. It was a small class. We took it for no credit. The instructor, my father, was able to get Marshall McLuhan, Edward R. Murrow, Charles Collingwood, and Gabriel Heatter to come as guest lecturers. They came at their own expense. They were thrilled that somebody cared enough about television to teach a course on it. The first time J. P. Costello showed unedited footage of John Kennedy's death, of Bull Conner and his boys turning clubs and dogs on Mississippi Freedom Riders, of the protests in Southeast Asia—monks setting themselves alight, or children, their clothes burnt off by napalm, running down the road—they cried. People vomited. People ran from those rooms to stage demonstrations in the street. Today, those videos just don't have the same effect. But the scene from *The Good Earth* does. I can't show *Old Yeller* or *Random Harvest* or Shirley Temple watching Victor McLaglen die without having half the audience in tears.

"In the last two years I have personally known several people who met with, well, violent ends—and as much as I regretted their deaths, I didn't cry for any of them the way I cried for poor Victor McLaglen.

"Today, a screenwriter in California was found dead in his hotel swimming pool. A man named Ralph Perrin. I didn't know him. I just talked to him once on the phone.

He seemed like a nice man. I don't know much about his career, but I know he wrote movies so I feel a loss. I hope in this class, this second half of the term, to show you what the American movie has taught us about ourselves. I hope you'll come away from this class not with a profound appreciation of me or of this course but of those filmmakers—many of them not very smart, not very nice people—and how they changed our world."

Jackie was too distracted to enjoy the rare tribute of applause after her lecture. In fact she was so busy getting ready to go home and collect her thoughts before continuing with good old Lieutenant McGowan that she very nearly blew off her student when the young girl came up to talk to her.

"Ms. Walsh?"

Jackie turned her head but started moving toward the exit. "Yes?"

"I really appreciated your lecture."

"Thank you," Jackie picked up her pace.

"About Mr. Perrin . . ." Lynn called out after her.

Jackie stopped at the door. She then took in the student, who she recognized as Lynn Bigbee, one of the roommates of a former student of hers, Danielle Sherman. "Do you know Mr. Perrin?"

"Well, he's in this book."

Jackie waited patiently as the young girl walked slowly up the aisle to her, holding an open library book.

"May I see?" Jackie asked, swiftly taking the book from her student's hands.

Jackie looked at the picture of the deceased screenwriter, turned to the cover—and then turned back to the short chapter on Ralph Perrin. Jackie could now see why Michael McGowan was playing it so strictly by the book, why the Palmer police were so nervous, and why the LAPD was going to such great lengths to solve the case. The book in her hands was *African-Americans in Show Business* and the picture showed Ralph Perrin to be a very attractive, very distinguished man, who happened to be black.

CHAPTER 8

When the young film instructor and her dog turned up the walk to the Walsh home, Jackie saw a hockey stick lying on her lawn. Flanking it were two hockey gloves. As Jackie push-buttoned her access code into the door lock and proceeded inside, she saw a long gym bag bulging with ice skates on the foyer floor. Moving farther inside, Jackie next saw a long blue hockey jersey dangling from the rail of her staircase and a pair of bulky padded pants lying on the doorsill into the living room. "Peter!" Jackie said brightly. "You're home."

Peter, decked out in exercise shorts and a torn Black Sabbath T-shirt, lay amid a pile of couch cushions, empty soda bottles, and nacho corn chips. He looked up from the blaring TV to say, "Hi, Jake!"

Jackie then swung her shoulder bag onto a hall chair and yelled, "Could I ask you turn that down, Peter?"

The redheaded eleven-year-old groaned, fished the TV remote control out from under his body, and then lowered the volume from "17" to "16."

"Any calls?!"

Peter snarled something that Jackie took to be no. He then threw a pillow at Jake too late to keep the big dog from stealing the last little bit of Monterey Jack cheese he was having with his chips.

"Peter! How was your sleepover at Isaac's?"

"What?"

Jackie went to the switchbox under the stairs and flipped a lever killing the circuit that ran the TV.

"Hey!"

Turning on the air conditioner (located on a different circuit) by her office space, Jackie then walked over to where her sprawled son lay fuming. "Peace and quiet. It's wonderful. Now, how was your sleepover?"

"Fine," Peter responded tersely.

"Were you polite?" Jackie asked, turning off the now useless television. "Did you say please and thank you?"

"Sure."

"Did you and Isaac decide to practice your hipchecks and destroy half the living room?" Jackie inquired as she put the cellular telephone back on its recharge stand.

"No. The only thing we broke was this chair and they said it was okay 'cause it was pretty old anyway."

Jackie grabbed her son from behind. "What am I going to do with you?"

"Choke me to death, I guess."

Jackie tickled Peter, which he pretended not to enjoy. "What happened to that sweet little boy I brought with me to Palmer? Was he kidnapped by aliens?"

"Can I watch TV?" Peter replied.

"No. Michael is coming over."

"All right! He'll watch TV with me."

"Not this time. He's coming on official business."

"Yeah?" Peter sat up and for the first time showed a little interest. "Someone else got whacked at the college?"

Jackie gave Peter a pretty wicked glare. "You're going to get whacked if you keep throwing things at Jake. Remember, he can get mean and I don't think he likes teenagers any more than I do."

Peter turned around and yelled, "I'm sorry, Jake. You shouldn't have glommed my cheese, but I'm sorry."

Jake, lying by the air conditioner, gave Peter a look, then went back to his slumber.

"I don't suppose," Jackie yelled as she went back out into the hall to restore the electricity, "that you're hungry for some real lunch?"

"Maybe Mike will bring pizza," Peter offered hopefully.

"I don't think so," Jackie yelled back as she went into the kitchen. "How long have you been here? Why didn't you fill Jake's water dish?"

"What's the point if he's not even here?" Peter wailed, following his mother into the kitchen. "Why won't you tell me why Mike is coming over? Did some murderer escape from prison?"

Jackie gave Peter the same look Jake had given him earlier. "If you must know, Mr. Nosey, a man Granddad used to know died in Los Angeles—perhaps under suspicious circumstances. I spoke to him on the phone the other day and Lieutenant McGowan wants to know what he said to me."

"Oh," Peter replied disgustedly. "Is that all?"

"Yes!" Jackie responded firmly. "Do you want some iced tea?"

Peter made a derisive face. "With no sugar?"

"There are plenty of packages of Almost Sugar on the table, dear."

"Yuch. Isn't that the stuff they were pouring in the water that almost poisoned everybody?"

"No, I don't think it is, Peter," Jackie answered. "Now I have some papers to look through so I want you to pick up all your stuff and put it away in your room. Then I want you to gather up your garbage and put the couch back the way it was. After that, sprint upstairs, wash up, and change into clean clothes. Then, when you're finished, rocket back down here and help me set the table."

"Why do I have to do everything?!"

"Well, why do you have to undo everything, Peter?"

"It isn't fair!" Peter howled.

"Tell me about it." Jackie then walked into her office and looked for the note that had been left on her door the night before. It was not on her desk. Jackie looked on her file cabinet, then in the wastebasket, then she looked around on the floor. "Peter!"

"Now what?!"

"Come here!"

Peter threw the couch cushions back down on the floor and came over to Jackie's office. "What?"

"Did you see . . . ?"

"I haven't touched any of your stuff, Mother. I know how psycho you get."

Jackie gave her son a narrow look. "Peter, this is important. There was a note here. A small piece of paper, like from a memo pad, and a small blank envelope with the top torn open. I have to show it to the lieutenant. It may be part of a murder investigation and I left it right here on my desk."

Peter spread his arms wide in outraged innocence. "What would I do with it?!"

"Are you sure you weren't in here?"

"Yes!" Peter shouted. "Ask Jake. Maybe he ate it."

"He doesn't eat paper, Peter."

"Yeah, well, he eats cheese."

"Not if you fill his bowl and water dish like you're supposed to," Jackie responded quickly. "Okay. Listen. Go upstairs. Look around by my nightstand. Carefully."

"Yes, Mommy dearest," Peter replied, moving slowly off toward the staircase.

As Peter slogged off upstairs, Jackie checked the places she knew the envelope could not be—on top of the refrigerator, back on the phone stand, in her shoulder bag.

When Jackie heard a crash upstairs it just barely registered, so intent was she on trying to figure out where the note could be.

Peter then bounded down the stairs. "Not there."

"What broke?"

"I don't know. Some bottle. Lotion or something, I think."

Jackie counted ten, then said in an even tone, "Try and be more careful, Peter. All right. Go out in the backyard."

"Why?"

"Check around by my chair."

"Did you take it out there?"

"I don't think so, but I'm running out of places in the house to check."

All of a sudden Peter was hugging her. "Ma."

"What?"

"Don't worry. If it's here, it's still here, right? We'll find it."

"I hope so." Jackie was happy to feel her son's arms around her, despite her worry. "Okay, go, go. Mike will be here any minute and I still want you to change."

As Peter opened the back door for Jake to go out, Jackie once more went to her shoulder bag—this time riffling through the pages of Perrin's manuscript to see if she had used the card as a bookmark. No luck.

All of a sudden Jackie heard Peter shouting. "Ma!"

Jackie rushed into the kitchen. "Did you find it?"

"No!" Peter yelled, pointing out into the yard. "It's Jake. He's barking at something on the other side of the fence."

Jackie joined her son at the back door. "What is it? A dog or a cat?"

"Ma. Jake doesn't bark at cats."

Peter was right. Not like that anyway. Jake was furious.

"Go get him, Peter," Jackie instructed, reaching for Jake's seldom used leash. "Bring him in."

"Why's he doing that?" Peter asked. "Think he smells a burglar, like the last time?"

"I don't know," Jackie responded, pushing Peter outside. "Go find out." Jackie then walked over to her phone and picked it up. "Hello, Palmer Central Police Precinct. I'd like to report a possible prowler . . . Hello?" Jackie tried to talk, but she soon became aware of a blanket of static on the line. "Hold on," she said, moving with the cellular phone to another location. Jackie occasionally had troubles of this kind with her phone although it had never been this bad before.

"Hello?" Jackie was perplexed. Everywhere she went in her small apartment it was the same. A piercing static made any transmission over the phone impossible.

"Listen!" she said to the dispatcher who may or may not have still been on the line. "I'm having trouble with my phone. I'll have to call you back."

Jackie put the phone back in the recharger and was looking through the drawer in the hall table for more batteries when Peter came rushing back in. "Mom!"

Jackie turned, alarmed. "Where's Jake?"

"He's gone!"

"What?"

"I couldn't stop him," Peter panted. "Before I could get the leash on, he jumped the back fence and started running toward River Street."

"Damn it." Jackie was upset. "He was barking last night at the studio. Like someone was in there."

"What?"

"I know. It's supposed to be empty, but I didn't get too worried, because I thought some real estate person might have been showing the apartment. Maybe it was an intruder, because when I wanted to go out Jake insisted on going with me. He never did that before."

"Wow, it's like Jake is a bodyguard. Like Mr. T."

"Maybe." Jackie nodded nervously. "Or maybe I'm making this all up in my head."

"Well, you didn't make up that Jake was chasing somebody around back by the studio," Peter responded. "He got loco bananas, then jumped over the fence. I mean, that was something."

Jackie slipped the new battery into the phone receiver, then turned to her son. "Listen, Peter."

"What?"

"There may be a prowler in the neighborhood. This may have something to do with that man I told you about being killed. The prowler may be trying to get into our house. Or he may just be trying to scare us into keeping quiet about whatever it is he thinks we know."

Peter started to whoop with excitement but the expression on his mother's face helped him think it through. "This isn't so cool, is it?"

"No. It sure isn't."

"Think he's going to kill Jake like the guy did in *Cape Fear*?"

A tickle of terror crept up Jackie's spine. "Let's certainly hope not. Take a peek through the window."

Peter took a step toward the window and then stopped. "What if he's right outside?"

"Peter . . ."

"No, I'm serious. What if he's standing on the porch and when I pull back the drapes . . . ?"

"Peter," Jackie replied firmly. "This is not a Monogram horror picture. We are not going to see someone in a fright mask and go 'Woo! Woo! Woo!' and go hide under the bed. Whoever it is, they don't want us to see their face so we can testify against them. And I'm sure they don't want us to see them and arm ourselves with secret weapons."

"What weapons?"

"Did you bring in your hockey stick, like I told you?"

"Yeah. Oh, boy, you mean I get to high-stick him?"

Jackie put her hand on Peter's shoulder, gave him her blackest look, then said, "Just get it."

While Peter rushed down into the basement, Jackie went into the bathroom to try the phone again. Suddenly she heard a dull boom. Jackie looked up and saw cracks cobwebbing across the wall of her bathroom. Stifling the urge to scream, Jackie dropped the phone and started backing out of the bathroom.

Then something hit the wall again and Jackie saw a strange, dust-covered, thin, blue-steel face of a hammer come through her wall.

Almost tripping over her own feet, Jackie exited the bathroom. She pulled the hall table out into her pursuer's path, then rushed into the basement. Fortunately, the basement door had a lock. Throwing the bolt, Jackie rushed down the stairs.

Peter was waiting for her near the bottom of the stairs. He had his hockey stick. "What's the matter, Mom? Is he upstairs?"

"I think so," Jackie said breathlessly, holding on to her son's shoulders to keep from falling over.

"I'm going up," Peter announced, managing to keep his voice bass throughout the entire sentence.

"You're doing nothing of the kind," Jackie said firmly. "Come." She pulled Peter over to the window. "Can you crawl out if I give you a boost?"

"I think so."

"The next time you feel like eating an entire bag of nacho corn chips and cheese, remember today."

Peter gave his mother a glare, then grabbed for the sill. Jackie interlaced her fingers and grunted as she took the weight of her eleven-year-old.

"Higher!" he demanded.

"I'm doing the best I can, Captain," Jackie mumbled in her best Scots accent.

"I can't reach . . ." Peter grunted. "Can I step on your head, Ma?"

"No, thank you!" Jackie said loudly. "Here—let me change my grip." Jackie pushed up and Peter managed to grab on to the window.

"Got it." Slowly, painfully, Peter unlocked the catch and tugged at the window. Suddenly a face appeared in front of them.

"Aaagh!" Peter screamed, letting go.

Mother and son crashed to the ground, then Michael McGowan, the face at the window, called down to them. "Are you all right? If you let me in, maybe I can help."

Jackie was all right. A rip in her slacks and a couple of bruises were all that she had suffered. Peter had the wind knocked out of him, but otherwise was fine. After making sure mother and son were okay, McGowan got into the house, looked around, and then called for Jackie and Peter to come up. "Do you want to look around? Is anything missing?"

"I'll go upstairs and check my hockey cards!" Peter yelled.

Jackie took a quick look around. "Well, I can see one thing that's been taken."

"What's that?"

"The book manuscript I was reading."

"Why would someone take that?"

"Your guess is as good as mine."

McGowan nodded. "Where's Jake?"

"Why?"

"If someone planned to break in and knew Jake lived here, they may have done something to get him out of the way."

Jackie immediately ran to the foot of the stairs. "Peter! Come on. Let's go look for Jake!"

CHAPTER 9

While Michael McGowan filled out an official report, Jackie called the Cooks to make sure that Peter had gotten there safely and had been given dinner. Fortunately she didn't have to wait too long before Jason Huckle, DVM—a kind, caring young vet who Jackie had taken Jake to for treatment the first time mistress and dog had met—called her into the room where Jake was being attended to.

Jackie stared down at Jake, sick and heaving on the operating table. She then looked anxiously to the handsome vet whose immaculate blond Fu Manchu mustache was covered by a surgeon's mask. "What do you think, Jason?"

Huckle nodded. "He'll be all right."

"Which is more than you'll be able to say if I get ahold of the bastard who maced him." Jackie soothed the fur on Jake's heaving sides.

Huckle quickly but gently removed Jackie's hand. "I wouldn't touch Jake without rubber gloves, Jackie. That stuff will play havoc with your skin and you may accidentally transfer it to more sensitive areas of his body."

Jackie bit her lip as Jake shivered again. "How long will it be before . . . he's okay again?"

Huckle patted Jake's head as he delicately daubed at the Alsatian's nostrils with a long, cotton-tipped swab. "He's a hardy old guy. As soon as his nose and eyes clear, he'll feel a lot better. There's no permanent damage done."

"Thank God."

Huckle nodded again and rubbed the back of his own neck as if trying to knead away tightness. "If you or the police do turn up the can of whatever was sprayed on Jake, give me a call just in case. If it's a mace product I'm not familiar with, I might ask you to read me the ingredients or drop it off with me for my collection. Some of the mail order 'dog repellents' have 2-4-D and 2-4-T in them."

"What's that?"

"Agent Orange, basically. Even worse actually." Huckle removed his mask and Jackie could see the anger in his yellow-flecked green eyes. "I don't see too much 2-4-T toxicity in my line of work, but you read about it in journals."

Jackie swallowed painfully. "What happens if . . . ?"

Huckle's reassuring tone immediately returned. "Again, please don't worry. If Jake was doused with that sort of mace, we'll want to watch for jaundice or a swollen or enlarged liver, but it's not that strong a possibility."

"I hate this," Jackie said savagely.

"I do too," Huckle admitted, taking off his mask. "I've written several letters to magazines who sell pocket mace and advertise it as 'a safe and effective dog repellent.' I tell them just how safe and effective these products are to dogs and people. I tell them how even if used under the most optimum conditions against large and dangerous wild dogs—and let's face it, in this age of leash laws and apartment pets, how many large wild dogs is the average person going to encounter? But anyway, unless you catch a dog just right and empty one of these small four-ounce cans in its eyes and nose, you are not going to stop a charging animal. In fact, you are likely to make a bad situation a great deal worse. I mean, a mace-maddened dog is not likely to stick out its paw and want to shake your hand for helping to curb its antisocial impulses."

"I see what you mean."

"And mace is terribly unpredictable," Huckle continued. "How many people have taken off the top and pushed the button without seeing which way the nozzle was pointing? How many have sprayed it into the wind and had it blow back into their own faces? Or had it leak or explode while carrying it around in a pocket or a bag? How many innocent law-abiding people have actually been saved from mad dogs because they carried around a can of spray mace? I would bet you can count them on one hand. Do you know who buys 'doggie mace'? Criminals, sadists, and idiots and not necessarily in that order. They call some of these things 'The Mailman's Friend' but your average post office employee knows damn well that he's going to have a lawsuit on his hands if he decides to spray somebody's pet while he's on their property. No, this stuff is used by sadists who love to see animals in pain. They get their jollies exerting their power over harmless strays or other people's dogs. Then they try to justify their actions by claiming that the neighbor's dog was barking too much or digging in their garden. You even see idiots who use these on their own dogs to punish them for chasing cars or snitching plates of cookies off the table. Horrible stuff."

Jackie set her jaw. "It does sound horrible."

Huckle nodded again and led Jackie into the outer office. "What can you do, though, really? There are no federal or state laws against harming animals except in a couple of cases where police animals or military dogs are protected. Some towns have felony laws against someone coming into your house and killing your pet, but the moment the pet is off your property, or if your pet somehow survives the attack, even if it's crippled or blinded or maimed for the rest of its life, the action automatically becomes a misdemeanor. Most times you're lucky if you can get a policeman to write them a summons."

"Oh, if I catch the person that maced Jake," Jackie said assuredly, "I know where I can find a cop who will write them a ticket."

CHAPTER 10

With Jake being boarded at the vet's and a banged-up Peter boarded at his father's house, Jackie jumped at the chance of getting out of her own home for a few days. Even if it did mean traveling to Los Angeles with the overly protective Michael McGowan.

"You got your seat belt fastened?" he asked her for the third time.

"Yup," she responded. Jackie figured that if he was intent on acting like Jean Arthur, she would respond like Gary Cooper.

"There may be some turbulence over Utah, but other than that, according to *USA Today* we should be just fine."

Jackie desperately wanted to be annoyed at the lieutenant who had followed her around like a puppy dog ever since the break-in, but he looked so cute in his forest-green turtleneck and black slacks that she relented and smiled. "Fly much do you, Lieutenant?"

"Not since I was in the service," McGowan admitted quickly.

"And that was a few years ago," Jackie surmised.

"Almost twenty," McGowan replied tightly.

"Relax, Mike." Jackie smiled. "I have it on good authority you're in more danger sitting around your own home having an iced tea."

McGowan stopped worrying about the wings shearing off

and turned to Jackie. "Tell you what. I won't worry about
flying and you don't worry anymore about burglars."

"Why's that?"

"I've talked to the department and we're taking over the
studio in your duplex."

"What?" Jackie now tore herself away from the lovely
night-sky view outside of her porthole and gave the lieutenant
her full attention.

"It's not just for your benefit," McGowan explained.
"Although that's my main concern, frankly. You see, the
department rents hotel suites or small apartments as a matter
of routine. It's where we stash witnesses when we put up
visiting firemen and out-of-town applicants."

"Firemen?"

McGowan laughed at the expression on Jackie's face.
"Well, not literally firemen; these are out-of-town cops who
are coming to Palmer to give us information, or maybe
they're following some Palmer citizen who committed his
crimes in another town or looking for some fugitive holed
up in our fair city. And we get policemen or journalists from
other cities, sometimes other countries . . ."

Jackie laughed.

"What's the matter?"

"I'm just picturing German policemen watching enthralled
as the intrepid Palmer police sweep down on the All Night
Stop And Go in a daring raid to snag teenaged beer drinkers."

McGowan managed a small laugh. "Well, we're not that
hick, Jackie. I mean, we do get an occasional murder or
burglary, or drug ring, as you know."

As McGowan went on, an elderly couple seated in the row
ahead of them started to listen in.

"I'm sure we're not the first on anybody's list of great
police departments, but we do have most of the equipment
you see in Detroit or Chicago. And, from the point of view
of visitors, it's probably a little safer to ride around in one
of our police cars."

McGowan stopped for a moment as the older woman in

front of him asked, "What did he say?"

Her husband whispered, "He said something about taking someone for a ride in a police car. Joyriding, most likely."

A little unnerved, McGowan continued, "And we actually have had a couple of programs over the years that drew interest from the big cities. For instance, since we're located on three rivers, we've always had one of the best dive teams in the country . . ."

"Die teams?" the female eavesdropper asked her companion.

"Dive teams!" McGowan repeated loudly. "We were probably the first police department in the country to use diving dogs . . . like Jake."

"Who's Jake?" the woman asked.

"Probably that friend of his he took joyriding in the police car," the old man speculated. The elderly couple then went back to their checkers game leaving McGowan to continue uninterrupted.

"Lot of people have come to Palmer just to observe that. And we were one of the first departments to fingerprint schoolchildren when the missing kids thing got so serious. We bought the old bookmobile from the library system and refitted it into the 'Safety Trailer.' Now we drive that from school to school and set up on the schoolyard and fingerprint kids during recess and give 'em safety lectures. That was a good program."

"I know, Michael." Jackie smiled, touching the policeman's arm. "I was just teasing you, really."

"I know, I know," McGowan grumbled. "I sound like a spokesman for the Palmer Kiwanis here, but you know, we do get a little sensitive about being referred to as 'County Mounties' or 'Cops in Cat Hats' all the time. We've got our problems, like everyone else, but we really are trying. Especially since our old chief, Hero Healy, is back in charge."

"He's the one who's leaning on you to go strictly by the book?" Jackie asked.

"Well, not just me," McGowan replied, tossing some smoked almonds into his mouth. "Everyone. Too many free-lancers, too many eccentrics, too much corruption in the old days under Stillman. It got to the point where if I wanted a missing persons report I had to bribe the sergeant who worked there. Can you imagine?"

Jackie tried to change the subject. "Well, that was all during the tainted water days."

"Yeah, and I'm sure that's going to be Stillman's defense in front of the corruption board. But come on."

At that moment, Jackie spotted the air hostess with the beverage cart. "Do you want a drink, Lieutenant?"

"Yeah, I sure do." McGowan reached into his pocket.

Jackie reached for her purse.

"I got it," McGowan announced, putting his hand on her arm.

"Michael . . ."

"This is on the department, I mean. This isn't you and me as private citizens taking in the great wine vineyards of south-ern California. We're going to Los Angeles to assist their police department in the execution of their duties. Which means 'We fly, Palmer buys.' "

McGowan ordered a German beer, Jackie opted for a glass of white wine.

"I'm not sure how I feel about my tax dollars going to pay for drinks," Jackie remarked.

"I used to work security for the City Council," McGowan responded. "Trust me, you don't want to know what your tax dollars pay for."

"Remind me to tell you about this film I teach called *Mr. Deeds Goes to Town*."

"Sorry," McGowan teased, pouring his beer. "I don't watch anything that doesn't have nude scenes or color."

"Is *that* why they didn't have nude scenes in the thirties?" Jackie joked back. "They were waiting for color?"

McGowan gave the air hostess a five-dollar bill and apolo-gized because he didn't have anything smaller. The hostess gave him a look for a moment, thinking that maybe he expected her to laugh because he was kidding, then informed the lieutenant that there wasn't going to be any change.

"You're not in Kansas anymore," Jackie remarked. "We were talking about your department becoming my neighbor."

"Great idea, hunh?"

"Well, I like the idea of having out-of-town policemen within screaming distance. I guess I could learn to scream 'Help' in a few other languages, but who else would be sharing my humble abode?"

"Oh, an expert witness now and then. Sometimes the DA has to put up someone from out of town."

"Well, I've always wanted to learn more about cigarette ash," Jackie threw off lightly as she sipped her wine. "Who else?"

McGowan ticked them off on his fingers. "Applicants for the force. We recruit in twenty cities now."

"Trying to get minorities?"

"Yeah, and college graduates."

"Who else?"

McGowan's voice dropped slightly as he confessed, "People the FBI wants to hide."

Jackie's eyes narrowed. "Tell me you're kidding."

"No," McGowan said quickly, "but not all the time. Maybe never. It's just that . . . when the FBI wants a favor . . . it's good to give it to them. They're a great organization to have owe you a favor."

"I don't like that at all, Michael," Jackie said firmly. "I'm serious."

"These guys are not the criminals, Jackie. They're the witnesses. The good guys. Rats, but good rats."

Jackie was not the least bit mollified. "What if somebody decides to kill these rats, a bad cat, perhaps, with a nice messy bomb?"

"Jackie . . ." McGowan put down his beer and leaned over so he could look directly into her eyes. "It's like this. I know it's not perfect, but it will bring you a little more protection.

I'm doing this because I love you and I don't want anything to happen to you."

He then kissed her.

When it finally ended, Jackie looked at McGowan for a long moment. "So there may be turbulence over Utah, you say?"

"Yeah," McGowan responded. "After that, it's clear sailing."

CHAPTER 11

The Montrose Hotel in West Hollywood was nice. You could still see the wreckage from the riots but it was not right under your nose. The suite reserved for Jackie and McGowan was, as he had hoped, paid for by the Los Angeles police department.

McGowan fully expected to spend the night on the couch. In fact, he was nearly asleep when Jackie tiptoed in after him.

"Are you coming in?" she asked.

"Oh, boy," he responded.

"I figured . . ." Jackie explained, "we do like each other. And we do want to. So we might as well find out here if this is going to work out. So if it doesn't, we can go home, you know, and pretend like nothing happened."

"Oh, boy," McGowan said again, stuck for an answer. "Listen, you want to crawl in here, so if you do want to bail out you've still got a nice bed to go to?"

"Okay."

Jackie and McGowan were then together on the couch.

"You know," she said. "You're much softer out of your clothes."

"Thanks a lot."

"No, I mean . . ."

"What is it exactly that you're trying to say?" McGowan interrogated her. He was smiling, though.

Jackie took a deep breath, then said, all in a rush, "If you get weird after this and start ordering me around or pushing for a commitment or start getting superprotective on me, I'll kill you."

They looked at each other.

Jackie broke first. "What's the matter?" she giggled.

"I'm kicking myself."

"Why?"

"I knew I should have brought my Kevlar vest."

The next morning found Jackie at the motel swimming pool. She was just about to knife the water, when all of a sudden a terrible thought occurred to her. Jackie picked up a poolside phone and dialed her phone extension.

"McGowan," said a very sleepy voice.

"Hello, tough guy. It's me."

"Wha . . . Jackie . . . where are you?"

"By the pool. Listen. This isn't the same hotel where . . . ?"

"What? No, no. That was some cheap joint in North Hollywood. Enjoy your swim."

"I will. Mike . . . ?"

The lieutenant's voice grew stronger as he became more fully awake. "Yes, Jackie?"

"Last night was wonderful. Especially after we moved to the big bed."

"Yes, it was."

"When do we have to leave?"

"I'll come get you in about twenty minutes."

"Okay." Jackie hung up the phone with a sigh. Well, she joked to herself. If she was going to have a cheap tawdry fling, this was the town for it.

The shiny silver doors of the new Los Angeles Mass Transit Unit opened with a pleasant tone that reminded the riders of the opening bars to "Hooray for Hollywood."

The train cruised along and the out-of-towners found themselves at their stop in no time. As they walked down the steps, McGowan looked so irresistible in an open-necked blue and white striped shirt and gray pants that Jackie, wearing a yellow sundress, actually walked hand in hand with him for a few blocks.

The sight of the West Hollywood Precinct house, however, with its boarded-up windows, burn scars, and the American flag hung upside down on the flagpole (the international distress call for "Help!") sobered up the happy lovers. By the time they were buzzed into the Plexiglas-lined hall, in fact, they were once again nervous witness and visiting fire-man/out-of-town hick cop.

A massive Hispanic sergeant whose name badge identified him as "Lavan," holding what looked to be a mastiff on a choke chain, greeted them at the first desk.

McGowan's hand lightly touched Jackie on the small of the back, as if to reassure her. "Lieutenant Michael McGowan of the Palmer police department, here with Ms. Jacqueline Walsh. We've come to Los Angeles to aid Detective Sergeant Bryan Ivie in a homicide investigation."

Sergeant Lavan nodded. "Are you carrying a service weapon with you, sir?"

McGowan shook his head.

"Very good." Lavan then turned to Jackie. "Ma'am, if you'll please just put your bag on the floor in front of Strausse here. Don't worry, she won't destroy anything."

The sergeant then gave them a quick pass with the metal-detecting wand. He signaled to Jackie that she was clear and the dark-haired film instructor started to remove her shoulder bag. Jackie put it down in front of the big dog. The sergeant, having cleared McGowan, then went to the wall phone to inform Detective Ivie his guests had arrived.

"Welcome to Outland," McGowan joked in a passable Sean Connery accent.

"Yeah, well, ever since the first *Terminator* movie we've been prepared for anything," Lavan joked back.

Jackie didn't share the joking, because it was clear that Strausse didn't like something about her bag. "Uh . . ."

Lavan put his hand on Strausse's massive neck. The big dog was now making some ominous sound deep in her throat.

"Strausse," the big sergeant said again. The dog settled back.

"I don't have any guns or drugs or anything," Jackie said quickly. "Honest."

"I believe you, ma'am. May I?" Lavan picked up the bag, sniffed once or twice, then gingerly shifted things around, then said, "I know this is kind of personal. But your dog didn't get maced fairly recently, did he?"

The dog vibrated in some low register again.

Jackie looked wonderingly at Strausse, then turned back to the sergeant. "Yes, he was."

"In connection with Detective Ivie's case?"

"We think so," McGowan responded.

Lavan set his jaw and Strausse almost immediately copied his partner. "You need help, ma'am, bringing in this fellow who did that, you give me a call." The big sergeant took a business card out of a battered blue plastic folder and handed it to Jackie. "Day or night. On duty or off. I'll come. I'll come and I'll bring Strausse."

Following the big sergeant's directions, Jackie and McGowan walked up to the small office of Bryan Ivie. The young homicide detective, a small-featured, prematurely balding but still very handsome man, rose to greet them. "Welcome to Los Angeles," he said.

Jackie would have sworn, although she didn't know the man, that there was a twinkle in his eyes.

After quickly rehashing her phone conversation with Perrin, and the break-in of her house, Jackie settled back with a delicious cup of LAPD coffee.

"So, the lieutenant tells me you lost a manuscript that may have a bearing on this murder case of mine?"

"Well, I didn't lose it. Someone maced my dog and broke down a wall of my house breaking in to take it."

"Uh-hunh." Ivie was obviously unimpressed. "And this was actually the second burglary of your house?"

Jackie thought for a moment, then saw what the detective meant. "I guess so. It's not until you pointed that out to me just now, that I thought about it, but you're right. The burglar, whoever he was, must have gotten in Thursday night and removed the note."

"Why didn't he take the manuscript at the same time?" McGowan asked.

"I had it with me," Jackie replied.

"But we're assuming that the note was a forgery," McGowan pointed out, "and that the burglar had to get it back for fear someone could then recognize his handwriting."

"That's a possibility," Ivie confirmed. "At this point we don't know what happened. Ms. Walsh, according to your statement, the note could have gone up anytime between the time you left your house around nine A.M. and when you came home around six P.M., your time. Is that correct?"

"Yes it is," Jackie confirmed.

"Well, obviously it was physically possible for Ralph Perrin to get to Palmer, leave you a note, and come back here to meet his murderer. Mr. Perrin, according to our time frame, was killed somewhere between one o'clock Friday afternoon and three A.M. Saturday morning."

"But why would Perrin go to so much trouble?" McGowan asked. "To fly to Palmer to leave a note requesting a meeting he knew he wasn't going to be able to attend?"

"We don't know what happened, Mike," Ivie replied. "Maybe Perrin flew to Palmer, checked into a hotel, left a note for Ms. Walsh here . . ."

"Jackie is fine."

Ivie acknowledged the friendly gesture with a smile, then continued, " . . . then was lured back here to be killed."

McGowan accepted the possibility. "Have you tried to trace Perrin's movements?"

"We're working on it," Ivie replied, rubbing his high fore-head tiredly. "This fare war has made the whole process a nightmare. A one-way ticket from LAX to Palmer was eighty dollars cash—more if you used a credit card. You have to give some kind of name when you make your reservation, but they don't ask for ID. That means you can fly under any name you want. Worse than that, a lot of the fare deals are standbys. The airlines don't make a big effort to figure out who didn't show up for the flight and who took over the reservation. We've got someone working on it, but it'll be a miracle if we can establish that Perrin did or did not take a flight to Palmer and back."

McGowan indicated his sympathy. "Buck up, Bryan. We're trying on our end too—to see if we can establish if Perrin took a one-way flight out of Palmer. But it's like you said—it's no walk in the park."

"What about Perrin's hotel?" Jackie asked.

Ivie started to say something, then changed his mind. "We'll get back to that. Jackie, uh, about the manuscript. Now just how much did you read before it was stolen from you?"

Jackie shrugged. "It's hard to say . . ."

"Bryan."

Jackie returned the detective's smile. "Bryan, since I didn't have time to read the whole thing, I just skipped around. It's hard for me to think that there could have been anything in Mr. Perrin's manuscript that would cause someone to go to such great lengths to stop him from publishing. It was reprinted articles, mostly, about a film director who lived a long time ago. And from what I could tell, she just wasn't all that controversial."

Ivie shrugged. "This is Hollywood, lady. You'd be surprised what people kill each other over." And so saying, the detective closed his notebook.

"All right, I know you people have to get back, so let's go down to the property room. I'll show you what Ralph Perrin had on his person when he died at the Sun Ray Hotel."

As they left the office, Jackie asked, "Where was his permanent address? Here in Los Angeles?"

Ivie shook his head impatiently. "We haven't located it yet. He only had enough clothes with him for a couple of days, so he definitely has another residence somewhere."

As they stepped aside to allow a civilian police worker in a wheelchair to pass, McGowan asked, "Have you been able to find out if he had any enemies here?"

"At the risk of starting another riot," Ivie replied. "I would have to say this particular gentleman has a great and impressive wealth of enemies."

"Such as?"

"Ms. Walsh . . ." Ivie's eyes traveled to some of the other people passing in the corridor as if to explain his resumption of a more formal tone. "We are going to give you the opportunity to talk to a couple of people—individuals in the film and academic community who we hope will be more comfortable talking to you than they are talking to us. They will tell you things and then we'll talk again before you go."

The elevator arrived and they stepped aboard. Ivie ran his badge's security strip across the control, clearing it, and then pushed SB for the subbasement. "I tend not to voice my suspicions, especially early on in a criminal investigation, because the truth is, I suspect everybody."

McGowan and Jackie exchanged looks and obviously wondered if Ivie was kidding.

"Go ahead and laugh," Ivie replied. "If this makes you think I'm one of these Nixon Secret Service control freaks, well, that's the chance I take. But after seventeen years in this job, I see potential murderers where other people see Mahatmas and saints."

"But that doesn't mean you condone . . . ?" McGowan clarified.

"Pulling people out of their cars and beating the crap out of them?" Ivie finished. "No, of course not. I'll tell you folks. As crazy and as stupid and as opportunistic as the riots were, we got the message. We really did."

The elevator doors opened in a cold, dark, blue-painted concrete and steel corridor.

"What's this?" McGowan asked. "The morgue?"

"Property Department!" Ivie yelled. The sound of their shoes on the concrete floors made an awful racket.

"Why is it like a nuclear bunker?" Jackie asked.

"We look around, the three of us," Ivie explained, "and we see storage rooms where evidence is kept. Nothing very exciting, right? I mean Hollywood West doesn't even have a Macabre Museum like most of our sister precincts."

"Macabre Museum?" Jackie asked. "That sounds like a Roger Corman movie."

"Life out here is a Roger Corman movie," Ivie commented. "Actually, most of these little 'museums' are pretty rinky-dink. A couple of the actual murder weapons people used to kill someone—or a pair of false teeth with blood on them, or something."

"Lovely."

"But why do property rooms have so much security?" McGowan asked.

"Unfortunately," Ivie explained, "some people—cops among them—look around and see this place as Fort Knox or El Dorado or something. Those lockers over there contain a lot of junk, but they also hold millions of dollars' worth of property, including two vaults filled to the top with money—counterfeit and the real green; guns—just about anything you can think of, from secret Pentagon prototypes to Revolutionary War flintlocks . . ."

"Really?" McGowan said with a chuckle.

"Hey, I've seen squirt guns modified to fire .38 hollow-point slugs."

"Jeez."

"Yeah," Ivie responded. "The worst of it is drugs. We get easily ten million dollars' worth of drugs through here each year. And you know how much of a problem that's been for other departments. New York, Miami, Washington—cops getting caught stealing, dealing, substituting powdered sugar for cocaine so some drug lord can beat the gas chamber. This is the West Hollywood solution—'Goodies Jail.' "

"It looks sort of like Jack Benny's vault," Jackie remarked.

"That's a hot one." Ivie grinned. "I'll have to tell Rubinsteen. He'll want to put in a moat."

At that point they reached a wall of bulletproof glass with shielded pass-throughs and an intercom speaker. Ivie held up his badge.

A thin, small black woman in uniform looked up and then smiled. "Detective Poison! How they hangin'?"

"Don't say anything about hanging in this town, Officer Raines," Ivie instructed. "Let me have the box on Perrin, Ralph NMI. Homicide 771 of this year, *s'il vous plaît.*"

"Coming right up," Raines responded. "You want fries with that?"

The officers laughed. Jackie was dazzled by it all. "This place is really amazing."

"You should see the Hollywood Hills Precinct," Ivie remarked.

"Why don't we see any of this in movies?" Jackie asked.

"It's like when the Soviets used to get courtesy inspections of the fleet," Ivie explained. "The admirals would always bring them to our oldest ships. We're the same way with the TV and motion picture people. We only let them see the dinosaur museums downtown. We got enough troubles without giving the Crips and Bloods a guide map of our precincts."

Raines then returned with a large safety-deposit-sized see-through plastic box. "Here you are, Detective. I'll need a palm print and a signature."

As Detective Sergeant Ivie went to the counter against the far wall and put his hand on a computer touch screen, Officer Raines opened the thick Plexiglas hatch on her end. She then put the box into what looked like a dumbwaiter. Not until the officer put down the door on her side and relocked it could Ivie open the door on his side. He pulled the box out, signed the clipboard, then locked the hatch on his side.

"Merci beaucoups," he said.

"We're here to serve," Raines replied.

Ivie then led Jackie and McGowan to a room at right angles to the desk, a paneled room with large tables and comfortable chairs.

"They let you out of sight with it?" McGowan asked. "Or are there security cameras?"

"There are security cameras aplenty," Ivie confirmed. "And the boxes are automatically weighed and photographed going out and coming back in."

McGowan shook his head. "I'll tell you, Bryan. I'd be embarrassed to show you how simple our procedure is compared to yours."

"There's nothing to feel bad about," Ivie assured the out-of-town policeman. "You know, we get used to all this, but you think we wouldn't like an easier system? It's just that we have to keep track of a whole lot more people. How big is the Palmer force? Hundred, hundred twenty people?"

"Something like that," McGowan admitted.

"We have ten times as many. And about a quarter of this department turns over every year."

"That many?" Jackie asked, surprised. "Why?"

"Lot of reasons," Ivie replied. "The usual—retirements, sickness, better jobs, moves, burnouts. And some LA reasons. Cops here solve a case or two and become movie stars. Movie consultants, anyway. And people get hurt on the job. Over two hundred injuries last year. A lot of shootings. A lot of knifings. A lot of beatings. We do it, and we get a lot of bad publicity. Probably justifiably so. But I'll tell you, they aren't shy about beating up on us when they get their opportunity."

Ivie then opened the box. "Perrin was dressed in a pair of brown linen shorts, a white, oversize, button-down cotton shirt, and a pair of brown sandals. That sound familiar to you at all, Ms. Walsh?"

Jackie shook her head.

"You've probably seen pictures of the deceased by this time. In case they're out-of-date—at the time of Ralph

Perrin's demise, he was a seventy-two- or seventy-three-year-old African-American male with light brown skin, about five feet ten inches in height, weighing approximately two hundred and sixty pounds. He had black curly hair with male pattern baldness." Ivie gave the others a wry smile, then continued, "Large-boned, big hands and feet. Facially, he had a full set of teeth, mostly his own, salt and pepper eyebrows, white sideburns, and a medium-length beard, mostly gray. He had a tattoo of a naked woman holding a sword on his right forearm and wore a heavy, dull silver bracelet on his left arm. No watch. He wore a leather thong necklace around his neck with a single dog tag with his name and blood type on it and a small assortment of colored wooden beads. Mr. Perrin was actually barefoot when found in the water, but they found one brown leather sandal near the body, which was found to fit the corpse and was presumed to be his. Other than the jewelry, Mr. Perrin had no personal effects on him when he was found. No money, no papers, no pens or pencils, nothing."

"Not even a room key?" McGowan inquired.

"He left it with the desk clerk," Ivie asked. "And before you ask—no, that's not a common procedure anymore. Mr. Perrin was either old-fashioned or particularly trusting."

"Also he didn't have any pockets in his shorts," Jackie pointed out.

"Good point," Ivie conceded. "I'd better make a note of that."

McGowan looked in the box. "Now, what's all this other stuff? Whatever was in his hotel room?"

Ivie nodded. "What we came up with. No guarantees that he didn't have a whole lot more when he checked in. The Sun Ray is not what you might call deluxe security accommodations."

"Was there a wallet?" McGowan asked.

Ivie pointed to a battered brown-leather wallet, probably twenty years old. "No money. No credit cards. No driver's license."

"How was he going to pay the bill?"

"Well, that's a matter of some dispute," Ivie answered McGowan. "The desk clerk, Mr. Philley, a black gentleman of about the same age as the deceased, says that Mr. Perrin paid him on Thursday morning, his second day at the hotel. It is Mr. Philley's statement that Perrin paid him for the previous day, for that day, and for the following day, in cash, one hundred and twenty-three seventy. He doesn't recall whether or not he gave Mr. Perrin a receipt. We didn't find one among the effects. Mr. Philley says that he distinctly remembers that Mr. Perrin paid him from a small sheaf of bills held together with a money clip with a large Spanish coin on it. There is no sign of that money clip."

"Who's got another story?" McGowan asked.

"The manager. He doesn't know anything. According to him, Perrin didn't pay his bill and nothing was stolen from his room."

"It's probably silly to ask," Jackie interrupted. "But there wasn't any trace of the manuscript?"

"Actually, we found this." Ivie held up a large square polyethylene computer cover.

"Mr. Perrin had a PC," McGowan pointed out.

"It seems that he did," Ivie agreed. "He was even heard to ask if his hotel room had a three-prong adaptor so he could recharge his computer. What we can't absolutely establish is whether or not whoever killed him was the person who stole the computer. We can assume that's the case, but we can't be sure, unless we eventually find it in the possession of the murderer. So that's the crux of this part of the investigation. Any comments or suggestions?"

McGowan started to say something, but then saw that Jackie had a question and deferred.

"It seems odd to me, Detective," Jackie commented, "that this manuscript would have been typed on a personal computer."

Ivie opened his notebook to a fresh page. "Why is that?"

"So much of it," Jackie answered, "was reprinted material. Take it from a writer, it would be the most boring thing in the world to type long articles straight out of books into a personal computer. Especially"—she then pointed to the computer cover—"on something as cheap as this. Computers this old only let you type for an hour or two at a time. My bet, if there's any way you can track it down, would be that Mr. Perrin either had a typing service do that part of the manuscript, or had access to a bigger computer with a scanning device."

Ivie absorbed the suggestion and made a note. "Okay. Good thought. If he did hire a typing service, would he have used his own name?"

Jackie nodded. "I think so. Besides, his name and details about his career were sprinkled all through the manuscript. There wouldn't have been much point in hiding it."

"Makes sense," Ivie said, nodding.

Now it was McGowan's turn. "One thing about the computer bag bothers me. Why not take it too? The thief—whether the murderer or just a thief—would have been a lot more discreet leaving with something in a case, than carrying a computer without a handle in his arms."

"That's a good point," Ivie agreed. "But you see, we found the computer bag under the bed, partly stuffed with clothes."

"What?"

"Mr. Perrin apparently went to some trouble to make it appear like he was using this case as a laundry bag. But there's something else."

Jackie, sensing the next question would be directed to her, looked up alertly.

"Jackie, you said that based on your phone conversation and the cursory look you took through the manuscript that it was your impression that Perrin was knocking off this book just to make a few bucks?"

Jackie nodded. "That was my impression. He didn't come right out and say it, but he seemed awfully anxious that I should read it and pass it on to the University Press."

"And Jackie said before that Perrin's comments throughout the book indicated that he wasn't really all that thrilled by the woman he was writing about," McGowan added.

Ivie nodded. "Well, that all makes a certain amount of sense. Especially when you look at his possessions, which are inexpensive or well worn. But it opens up a whole new series of problems. How much was he going to make off this book? Not a whole lot I would guess."

Jackie shook her head. "Perhaps he would have made a decent amount eventually. Especially if the book became popular and was chosen as a textbook, but university presses traditionally aren't all that generous with their advances. They would have offered five hundred to a thousand dollars tops."

"That's all?" McGowan asked, amazed.

Jackie shrugged. "Remember, this is academia. Mr. Perrin had no academic standing. Most film professors writing this kind of book just do it to keep up their prestige in the academic community. The smart ones and the broke ones manage to get a grant from the government or some private fund for another three or four thousand. Then it's worth doing. I'm not sure how aware Mr. Perrin was of the whole situation, but there's no question that if he was hoping this book would bail him out of a tight financial hole, then he was in for a disappointment."

Ivie rapped on the table. "That's exactly what I suspected. So here we have some poor schmo, down on his luck in the industry, making little or nothing—maybe because of his age, maybe because he couldn't write today's pictures, or maybe because of who he was and all the enemies he made in the business. He writes this book, which presumably he spends some money researching, while he's sitting at home waiting for the phone to ring."

Jackie and McGowan showed by their expressions that they were with him so far.

"Yet from the time he talks to you on Wednesday, Perrin suddenly acts like he's got all sorts of money. He pays for his hotel room in cash the next day."

"And we have to wonder why he has to live in a hotel all of a sudden," McGowan contributed. "Forty bucks a night is cheap by LA standards, but you're not going to be able to keep that life-style up too long if you're writing library books."

Ivie nodded. Obviously the same thing had occurred to him. The detective sergeant then turned to Jackie. "You said you were willing to read the book and pass it on, if you could, but you said nothing to him that indicated that you were dying to see the manuscript. Is that right?"

"Absolutely," Jackie agreed.

"So you'd think he would have mailed it to you," Ivie mused aloud. "Maybe overnight delivery to make sure it got there all right. But I can't see faxing it which has got to be five or ten times as expensive."

"Unless he had a friend who could do it for him for free," McGowan suggested.

Ivie absorbed this. Clearly it was something he hadn't considered. "Well, I guess we should follow that up." Ivie then turned to Jackie. "When you get home, can you try to find out if the college kept a record of which number the fax was transmitted from?"

Jackie nodded.

"We may be able to get that from the phone company, but it'll be tough if he used one of these little long distance services that rent lines from AT&T. Their records aren't always the best. Anyway, he faxes the manuscript to you, which surprises you."

"Very much."

"And then, he flies to Palmer the next day?"

"Maybe," McGowan pointed out.

"Maybe," Ivie agreed. "But if he doesn't, someone goes to a helluva lot of trouble to make it seem like he does. Making hotel reservations, leaving you a note, then breaking in to steal the note, then killing Perrin so he can't be questioned."

"It's a strange case," McGowan agreed.

"It is indeed," Ivie agreed. "Listen, I still have plenty of questions, but you must be hungry. I know I am. And if I don't take lunch right now, I won't get it. Would you mind continuing this 'interrogation' at a seafood restaurant? The department will treat."

McGowan and Jackie exchanged looks. The young film professor was clearly willing. "Sounds great."

The traffic on La Brea was at least manageable; Ivie's Jeep Cherokee towered above most of the low-slung expensive sports cars.

"How do you like your Jeep?" Jackie asked. "I love mine."

"Gotta have them," Ivie averred. "The drug dealers have used them for years. They cut across dividers, drive on rocky shoulders, take right turns into the aqueducts. You've seen the movies. We try to stay with them. Drug dealers are like the Russians used to be, they keep forcing us to upgrade our equipment."

After a fifteen-minute ride, Ivie's Jeep pulled into the Marina Del Rey. The sign on the outside of the ramshackle old pier restaurant said Bob McHugh's SeaFood Shack.

"Here we are," Ivie announced. "Not a bad little place. Like Joe the BeachComber's used to be, and a whole lot closer. It's not cheap, but you can lunch here and leave with most of your arms and legs."

McGowan pointed to the cartoon likeness of Bob McHugh and asked, "Is that . . . ?"

"Yeah, the skipper from that lousy TV show. He's a nice guy but a bit of a blowhard. If you see him, don't do anything more encouraging than wave. If you're not careful, he'll pull a chair over to the table, start ordering rounds of drinks at our expense, and use up our entire lunch hour talking about his old TV acting days."

The trio walked inside, and were seated in the back near a fake shark head with a license plate in its mouth. They sat for a moment, ordered drinks, and enjoyed the atmosphere until the waitress came over. Then, ordering three helpings of maki maki to go with their bottle of white wine, Ivie brought the focus back to the case at hand. "Okay. I told you that the computer bag was half-filled with clothes. There was something else."

While his guests nibbled breadsticks and sipped their wine, Ivie took a Polaroid snapshot out of a plasticene envelope in his folder.

McGowan took the picture and then handed it to Jackie.

"Money," she said.

"Almost seventeen thousand," Ivie confirmed. "If he had it all along, it explains why he could afford to live in a hotel room and fax manuscripts and buy airplane tickets."

"Then why all this fuss about getting his book published?" McGowan asked.

Ivie looked to Jackie knowing she wanted to speak. "Go ahead."

"It's possible that Mr. Perrin was looking for a teaching job."

Ivie nodded. "That's what occurred to me too. Maybe because we're so used to seeing that here in southern California—someone in the industry who had a pretty good run gets into teaching after a while, figuring that if things pick up again they can always quit or take a leave of absence. Is there any reason though, Jackie, that he would have picked Rodgers University especially?"

"Well, he knew that my father did." Jackie thought for a moment. "I know that the U is always looking for qualified minority instructors but I'm not sure if *he* knew that. We get heat for having so few black professors although Dean Westfall maintains that very few qualified African-Americans ever apply."

"Anything else?"

"Well, this is a long shot, but I was told by the chairman of the Communications department where I teach that they had approved a new budget which would expand our

program. They were committed to hiring at least two more
screenwriting instructors. If Ralph had any kind of ability at
all he would have been perfect."

Ivie nodded enthusiastically. "Good. That's even better
than I hoped. You didn't happen to mention that to Perrin
during your phone conversation, did you?"

Jackie shook her head. "No, I told you what we discussed.
I didn't talk to my chairman until the next morning. It had
obviously been in the works for some time. I hadn't heard
rumors, but I'm sure others had. And I wasn't the first one
in my department told about the expansion plans."

"All right, so it's possible," Ivie concluded. "The reason
he may not have directly asked for your help in helping him
get on the faculty was that he may have already talked to
someone else. Perhaps someone with more clout."

Jackie favored the detective with a wry smile. "That
would be just about everybody. I'm an associate professor,
untenured. My recommending anyone, especially the sort of
lukewarm recommendation I'd be forced to give to someone
I'd never met, like Ralph Perrin, would have counted for next
to nothing."

Ivie nodded. "Another thing we found among Perrin's
possessions was an address book. It looked to be his main
address book. Binder at least twenty years old. The entries
were in no particular order. The pages were looseleaf. When
a page was getting pretty messy, he probably just copied the
ones he still needed on a fresh page. It'll take us a while to
sort things out. His handwriting and spelling aren't the best.
And there's the inevitable first or last name only entries, or
initials or some combination of the above, or an abbreviation
that we can't read. Perrin doesn't look to be the kind of guy
who would use any particular code, he just wasn't that well
organized."

Jackie shrugged. "I'd hate to have you see my address
book."

"Well, touché. I guess none of us are as organized as
we might like," Ivie admitted, finishing his last bite of maki

maki. "Anyway, I have several names and numbers relating to Palmer personalities. Do you know a Yelena Gruber?"

Jackie nodded. "She's in my department. An acting instructor."

"Keith Monahan?"

"He's another instructor in Communications—although he teaches in another building. He's also in charge of the college radio station."

"Jonathan Kersch?"

"He's also in my department," Jackie responded. "He teaches Theater Management and grant writing. Jonathan also recently became the deputy chairman of the department."

"And Ivor Quest?"

"The chairman of the department," Jackie answered easily. "And the famous director, of course. Until very recently he really hasn't spent that much time around the university."

Ivie nodded. "Here are some numbers, on one of the last pages. Your area code, of course. Do you recognize them?"

The detective moved an index card down, revealing the first number.

"No."

The card moved down a line to the second number. "How about this one?"

"The number's familiar, but I can't place it offhand."

Ivie then moved the card away completely to reveal the third number on the page. "How about that one?"

"Well, that's my mother's number," Jackie said quickly.

"Had it long?"

"Forever," Jackie responded at once. "Since my parents were married and moved into the Strang Arms Apartments in Palmer."

Ivie nodded. "The first number I showed you, Jackie, is a telephone booth in the bar of the Merrifield Travel Inn. Have you ever had occasion to use that phone?"

"No," Jackie responded, a little surprised by the question.

Ivie pushed his plate away from himself with a hard shove. "What if I were to tell you, Jackie, that you called that number from your house on Thursday?"

"I'd tell you there must be some mistake," Jackie replied. "I called the main desk of the Merrifield that night to talk to Ralph Perrin and left a message for him but . . ."

Ivie shook his head. "You called this number, Jackie. The Merrifield has no record of any reservation or communications with Ralph Perrin whatsoever. No record of talking to him. No record of talking to you."

Jackie's plate was whisked away by a silent busboy. "What are you saying?"

"Just that," Ivie replied in a flat tone, "the second number, Jackie, the one you thought was somewhat familiar, is your father's phone number in Palmer. According to the Screenwriters' Guild."

"Oh, his office line."

"You remember now?"

Jackie bristled a little at the detective's tone. "My father had a private line. My mother and I very seldom used it. We never gave it out to anyone. Of course my mother had it disconnected after my father died."

Ivie gave McGowan a look, then turned to another sheet of paper on his pad. "Jackie, these three numbers were found together on the last sheet in Perrin's address book. It looks to us as if Mr. Perrin didn't have your father's number and called the Guild. They gave him the last two numbers, the way they did when we called with the same request."

Jackie turned down the offer of coffee. Her stomach was bilious enough. "I'll guess I'll have to call the Guild and tell them my father's dead and not to give out my mother's number anymore."

"That may be a good idea," Ivie said noncommittally. "After your mother's number, Jackie. The last entry in the book is your name. And your number."

"It is listed in the book."

"But according to your statement, Mr. Perrin asked for you by your maiden name?" Ivie nodded at the waitress as his pound cake arrived.

"Yes," Jackie replied slowly.

"It looks to me, Ms. Walsh," Ivie continued, taking a big bite, "that your mother talked to Ralph Perrin and gave him your number."

"I don't know," Jackie responded. "That's possible, but if it's true, it's rather odd."

"Why would you say it's odd, Jackie?" Ivie followed up quickly.

"Well, for one thing when I mentioned Ralph Perrin to my mother on Thursday she acted as if she didn't remember him. He must have gotten my number another way."

"That's certainly possible, Jackie," Ivie responded, finishing his dessert. "But you see, Ralph Perrin made a number of calls from his room. The hotel charges for those calls and keeps a record. He did call the Guild. And he did call your mother's number. Now it seems to me to be a reasonable explanation that your mother gave him your number. Does that seem unreasonable to you?"

"No."

Ivie signaled for the check. "Is your mother a forgetful person? Could she have done this and forgotten about it afterward?"

"No!" Jackie responded at once. "My mother is as sharp as anyone you could name."

Ivie shrugged again. "Jackie, I am not trying to insult you or your mother. As I told you, I have a suspicious mind. Even when I don't suspect someone of murder I'm always interested when I feel someone's withholding information from me. And I wonder why they're doing it. Now why don't you . . . ?"

The waitress arrived with the check. Ivie gave her a credit card. The waitress walked away with it.

"If you would . . . call your mother? This evening or tomorrow. Talk things through with her. Try to find out what she knows and why she may have neglected to tell you before now. And then, get her to call me at this number." Ivie handed Jackie a card. She put it in her bag along with Sergeant Lavan's card.

"It's important, Jackie, that you make clear to her that this is a police investigation and that she should cooperate fully. If she doesn't call me in a few days, then I will call her. Okay?"

The waitress came back with the charge slip. When Ivie didn't immediately take it she put it down so close to his elbow as to be in the way.

"Now, as to the two people I want you to talk to today . . ."

"Just a minute," Jackie interrupted.

The waitress, tired of playing with crumbs she really didn't feel like removing, left them.

"What is it you think my mother knows?"

Ivie sat back and interlaced his fingers. "How intimately do you know your father's career, Jackie?"

The film instructor shrugged. "I guess there's a lot that I don't know. My father didn't marry my mother until he was in his late forties. I remember vaguely bouncing back and forth between apartments in Los Angeles and our apartment in Palmer when I was a little girl. My clearest memories of my father were as a Communications professor at the university. He didn't have a whole lot to do with Hollywood the last ten years of his life."

Ivie nodded. "Did he ever tell you why?"

"Not in so many words," Jackie replied. "He felt very removed from the current scene. They were doing disaster pictures and adaptations of stage musicals, which weren't my father's kind of thing. And he had a lot of bitterness, I think, about the way his last series fell apart."

Ivie turned to another page in his pad. The waitress came up a few feet, looked to see if Ivie's pen was going anywhere near the charge slip, then walked away disappointed.

"Jackie, one of our researchers spent some time at the Screenwriters Guild talking to people and reading through their files. One of the things she found was an incident that occurred in 1979. Do you recall the incident I'm referring to?"

Jackie shook her head.

"Your father and Ralph Perrin worked on a television movie and there was a dispute about credits."

"That often happens," Jackie replied, unconcerned. "Especially in TV. Residuals are paid on the basis of story credit, so writers take the matter to the Guild for arbitration. Most writers don't take it personally. I've been listed as coauthor on things where there were a half-dozen writers, none of whom I ever met."

"Well, as you say, Jackie"—Ivie moved a napkin across his mouth—"arbitrations are often routine and entirely friendly. This one wasn't, however. Apparently Mr. Perrin accused your father of taking a script he had submitted to your father's show, which was not bought, and adapting it into a TV movie, without giving him either payment or credit."

"That doesn't sound like Dad."

"It's a matter of public record, I'm afraid."

"What was the Guild's ruling?"

"A compromise was struck. Mr. Perrin was listed as a contributor in the credits and your father agreed to pay him some thirty thousand out of his fee for writing the teleplay. Is this something that would have been such a matter of routine to your father that he wouldn't have mentioned it?"

"No, of course not," Jackie responded. "He would have been furious. But he didn't say anything to me. He wouldn't have. Dad probably considered it part of the old *Tales of Justice* mess. That was a TV series he produced in the late fifties."

"One of my dad's favorites," Ivie volunteered.

"And," Jackie continued, "as I said, he was very bitter about the whole experience and he refused to talk about it to anyone. I think by the terms of the lawsuit, he was forbidden to."

Ivie expressed surprise. "He wouldn't tell his own . . . ?"

"When my father didn't want to talk about something, he didn't talk about it. Detective Ivie, there are a lot of people who sit around complaining about all the times they got screwed by Hollywood. And that's all they do. My father hated those kind of people." Jackie knew she was becoming emotional, but she didn't care. "My father spent forty years in and around Hollywood, writing scripts, producing TV shows, and when he walked away—that was it. He was very happy teaching Communications. And we almost never heard about his Hollywood buddies, let alone his enemies."

Ivie nodded. "All right, Jackie. I'm just making sure." The detective then signed the lunch check with a flourish and the trio got to their feet.

"You see, it occurs to me that perhaps Ralph Perrin, in his old age, was thinking about emulating your father. Taking a job at the same university, using this book of his to bolster his academic reputation, looking up old acquaintances who had ended up in Palmer."

As the detective continued to talk, the three people walked toward the exit. McGowan noted with some amusement that "The Skipper," Bob McHugh, was seated at a table with a bunch of tourists, as advertised, ordering drinks and launching one tale after another about his old TV series days.

"It looks to me," Ivie continued, "that this was what Mr. Perrin was trying to do, put his past behind him and start over again. But someone killed him before he could do that. Someone who held a very old, very serious grudge." Ivie held the outside door open for his guests. "And if it is someone you know who killed him, Jackie, I want your help to put him away."

Jackie reached for the sunglasses on her forehead and slipped them back over her eyes. The sun coming off the water was just brutal. "I want to help, Bryan. That's why I'm here."

"Good." Ivie pretended for a moment to fumble for the right key to open his Jeep door, then lowered the boom. "Because you see, Jackie, when people kill to cover up bad memories from their past, they usually keep on killing. And if I think you and your mother know more about Ralph Perrin than you're willing to say, the murderer has got to feel the same way."

CHAPTER 12

Ivie left Jackie and McGowan off on Hollywood Boulevard so that they could walk to their next destination. The couple moved along silently. McGowan, not knowing what to say, had decided to say nothing. Jackie's head whirled with the ramifications of what Ivie had told her.

Could her father really have stolen a script from this Ralph Perrin? Had her mother known? Was Perrin planning to blackmail her or her mother into helping him or giving him money? Jackie didn't suppose that such a scandal would cost her her job, but it certainly would have been unpleasant.

Palmer had always been a haven for her father—a place where he was a respected citizen, a beloved professor at the university, and yet still was able to maintain enough anonymity that he could go shopping or get a haircut without would-be actors approaching him in hopes of landing a role on one of his shows. To have those pleasant memories wiped out with an ugly smear would have been horrible. Who knows how her mother would have taken it? Could her mother have known all that when Ralph Perrin called?

Finally McGowan broke the silence. "Grauman's Chinese Theater," he pointed out.

"It's Mann's now," Jackie replied automatically.

"It seems so small," McGowan commented.

"It's more a matter that they tore down all the other theaters around it and put up big buildings instead."

"Want to go over? See how your tootsies stack up against Hedy Lamarr's?"

"I'm a size and a half smaller," Jackie lied. "But come on. Let's go look. I always like seeing Jimmy Durante's nose."

The couple looked at the footprints for a few moments. Many of them were sealed off now or covered with a thick transparent lucite slab that fit over the original sidewalk.

"You okay?" McGowan asked finally.

"Yeah." They walked past the used bookstores and when Jackie felt no urge to go in, she knew that she really wasn't okay. "Mike . . ."

"Yes, Jackie?"

"I don't care what anybody says. My father didn't steal a script. He couldn't have if he wanted to."

McGowan nodded. "Ivie's a strange egg. One minute he seems like a good guy. The next you wonder if it's all a 'good cop' act so he can sucker-punch you with the rough stuff. I don't know what to tell you, Jackie. I know, as another homicide cop, that it's an established tactic to take some story you hear somewhere, something you know damn well isn't true, and throw it out to see how the suspect will react."

"So, it's official. I'm a suspect?"

McGowan shrugged his shoulders. "If you are, you're not much of one. You've got an alibi for most of the time frame and it would be hard to get a jury to believe that you hired some guy to mace your dog and terrorize you and your son, just so you could make the manuscript disappear."

"Very hard, I would think. I find it hard to believe that there could be something in a book about a forgotten woman director that could cause someone to hack their way into my house through my bathroom wall just to get the manuscript. And surely my mother isn't a suspect for that."

"No, not really. But other people might find it possible that she hired someone else to do it. With your permission, I'll make a routine check of her bank records. If she has taken a large sum of money out recently, for instance the seventeen or eighteen thousand dollars that Ralph Perrin supposedly got, then we'll have to investigate further."

Jackie nodded. "My mother is a woman of strong emotions, Michael. I won't say she's not capable of murder, especially when it comes to defending me or my father's memory, but she is not the type to throw someone in a swimming pool. I mean, from the sound of it, Ralph Perrin was as big as a football player. It must have taken a strong person to hold him underwater."

"Jackie . . ."

"What?"

"Didn't you know?" McGowan saw the startled look on Jackie's face and then realized that she *didn't* know. "Ralph Perrin didn't drown. He was poisoned. I mean technically he may have drowned because the poison made him too weak to tread water, but somehow Ralph Perrin ingested a great deal of acetone."

"Acetone? That sounds like something to do with art products."

McGowan nodded. "It's used in a lot of things. A fixative or paint dissolver in art. It's used to clean film. It's used in all sorts of chemical products. You can buy it in any hardware store. They think the sort of acetone that was used to kill Ralph Perrin is sold in photography stores. Someone put it in a container of water along with something that gave it a slightly orange fragrance. It may have camouflaged the taste long enough for someone to drink a sufficient quantity of it."

"What's a sufficient quantity?"

"In a man like Ralph Perrin, with circulatory and respiratory problems? Not a whole helluva lot. He had more than enough in his body to kill him."

After several moments of watching tourists edge away from them, Jackie and McGowan realized that their very public talk of poisons was unnerving people.

McGowan smiled and gestured for Jackie to cross the boulevard. "Come on. We should really get over to the

DeLongpre address anyway. Before we miss this guy."

"Okay."

McGowan started across, but Jackie held him back.

"What? There's nobody coming."

"I know." Jackie smiled. "But they're very strict about jaywalking in California. It works both ways, they're equally strict about motorists driving through crosswalks while anyone is in them, even if the people have almost made it to the curb."

"Bloodthirsty Los Angeles tough on jaywalkers?"

"Everyone's got to draw their line somewhere."

"I guess."

"I know." Jackie smiled. "It seems silly, but it does work. I'm sure Los Angeles has fewer automobile-pedestrian fatalities than most cities. Now tell me about acetone. Doesn't this open up the time frame? I mean, Mr. Perrin could have had that doctored bottle of water for several days before he drank it. It might have even been some blind killing. Like the Tylenol killer."

"No, the police have ruled that out."

"Why?"

"I'll tell you in a minute. Let's cross." McGowan did a little gawking as he crossed the long street. "Isn't this where the La Brea tar pits are?"

Jackie looked off in the distance and pointed. "Way down there. See it? It's not really within walking distance."

McGowan gave an "oh, well" gesture. "Anyway, the acetone would have reacted with the plastic in the bottle if it was allowed to sit around for more than a few hours. So the doctored bottle was prepared no more than three hours before it was consumed. Also, the police are almost positive the murderer was with Perrin when he died."

"Fingerprints?"

"No," McGowan responded as they walked down the hot, cracked sidewalks—seldom repaired because they were seldom used. "It's more a matter of profiling. They're very big on that here. Feeding murder stats into a computer from a psychiatric profile. Poisoners almost always manage to be on the scene to watch their victims die. Partly it's a matter of sadism, I guess, or morbid fascination."

"What, to see what colors their victim will turn? Or how far out their tongue will hang?"

"Something like that." McGowan paused to wipe his brow. "Boy, this is like being in a microwave oven, isn't it? I should have brought some sunblock."

"I did." Jackie reached into her shoulder bag and pulled out a white tube.

"Thank you." McGowan started to rub the solution on his hands and face.

"You should really put some on underneath too," Jackie advised. "Don't worry, it won't stain and the sun really will go through that thin shirt."

"Okay." McGowan started to undo his buttons and then gave her a wicked smile. "Want to do my back?"

"Certainly not!" Jackie looked at the expression in McGowan's eyes and thought what a terror he must have been to little girls. "You."

McGowan then handed Jackie back her sunblock. "Thank you," he said in a grave voice.

Equally grave, Jackie replied, "You're welcome."

They found DeLongpre Avenue quickly, much to Jackie's surprise since she had not been to West Hollywood for seven years. The street was oddly reminiscent of a block on New York's Lower East Side, with its kosher butcher shops and its bagel shops and its sole Irish bar, a rarity in a town where people had gotten used to getting drunk at their dinner table. The building Jackie and McGowan were looking for was near Grace Street, a narrow, post-war, six-apartment structure with water closets, one for each apartment, at the ends of the halls.

Carefully waiting for the streetlight to change to the right color, they crossed and buzzed the bottom right-hand buzzer.

"Do you hear anything?" Jackie asked.

McGowan shook his head.

"You never know with these old buildings whether these buzzers work."

"He's supposed to be expecting us." McGowan shrugged. "Want to go in and knock on his door?"

McGowan looked at Jackie's hopeful expression and sighed.

The film instructor immediately took out a nail clip, flipped out the metal nail file that was absolutely useless except for purposes such as this one, and fit it in the lock.

McGowan then dug into his wallet and came up with his Palmer Pop-Eye Video card, a picture ID more sophisticated than the one the department had given him, and stood ready.

"Ready?" Jackie grinned.

"Ready," McGowan answered wearily.

Jackie pushed back the lock and McGowan slid his card down, holding the lock back. The heavy black-painted metal door pushed open.

Inside the vestibule they checked the names over the mailboxes. As with the buzzer box outside, no name was legible. In Los Angeles only actors put their names on outside buzzers and only writers put their names on mailboxes.

Jackie tried the file tip in the lock of the vestibule door. It opened easily. "Shocking," Jackie commented.

"We should call a cop," McGowan agreed.

The party they were looking for had an address of "B." The problem was, the doors were all set off at such strange angles it was nearly impossible to tell which apartment was "A" and which apartment was "D."

The couple split up and each checked two doors. They met again in a few moments in the center of the dark, uncarpeted hallway.

"See any letters?" McGowan asked.

"One of mine had a want ad taped on it saying 'Man Wanted.' The other had a peephole that somebody had drawn an eyebrow over."

McGowan nodded disgustedly. "The one in the back had a scratch and sniff taped over the peephole. This one's just painted black. Shall we go with the obvious?"

Jackie shrugged. "Why not?"

McGowan knocked on the black door.

The faint sound of the television inside was immediately extinguished.

They waited a moment to see if anyone would come to the door, then Jackie knocked loudly. "Hello? Is anyone there?"

They waited again, heard some scurrying inside, then they heard nothing at all. McGowan, now getting a little impatient, banged his fist on the door. "This is Lieutenant Michael McGowan of the police department. Would you open the door please?"

Jackie gave McGowan a look. "You don't have to knock his door down."

"I don't want to reach retirement age standing in the man's hall."

"You're just irritable because your collar is chafing your sunburned neck."

McGowan gave Jackie a look, then, infuriated because she was right, banged even harder on the door. "Hey you in there! I'm talking to you."

Finally a small quavering male voice made itself heard. "Who do you want? I didn't do nothing."

"We're looking for Apartment B. Official police business. Do you know which of these apartments that would be?"

"I don't . . . Listen, I'm sick," the voice whined. "You'll have to call the landlord. He lives in Santa Monica."

"C'mon, pal," McGowan demanded. "This isn't too hard. Just tell me which apartment is B."

"This is Apartment B," the voice wailed. "And I don't want to talk to you. Now leave me alone or I'm going to call Channel Six."

As McGowan sputtered, Jackie pulled his arm. "Come on. Maybe we have the wrong building."

They walked back out the front door and were looking for another building entrance when a young black man in his twenties pulled up to the corner, dismounted, and walked his bicycle toward where they were standing. The young man wore a black and silver warm-up jacket, cut off at the biceps, fingerless gloves, tight black Italian biking pants, and a pair of expensive black pump sneakers.

"Hello!" Jackie greeted him.

McGowan, still a little cranky, barked, "You Ralph Perrin, Junior?"

"I'm Ral Perrin," the young man replied. "Who wants to know?"

"We were just inside your building," McGowan grouched. "Which one is your apartment?"

"The back one on the left."

"B?"

"Yeah."

"Your neighbor said he lived in Apartment B."

Ral snorted. "That boy's some stone stupid vanilla-white liar."

"We'd like to talk to you for a few moments," Jackie said, consciously taking over for the still-scowling McGowan.

"You the police?"

"I'm Lieutenant McGowan," the sun-baked peace officer began, but Jackie cut him off.

"Michael and I are from out of town. We've been asked to assist the Los Angeles police on the investigation of the death of your father. Michael is a policeman, a lieutenant in the homicide division of the Palmer police department. I'm a film instructor at Rodgers University . . ."

"Really?" Ral's head jerked up with sudden interest. "You know Fred Jackson?"

"Why yes I do." Jackie smiled, a little surprised. "He teaches cinematography in the same—"

"That's what I do," Ral interrupted.

"Well." Jackie smiled. "That's very interesting. Would it be possible to go somewhere and talk for a few moments?"

Ral fiddled with the handlebars of his bicycle for a moment, then decided, "All right. It's too hot in my crib, let's check out the park."

Dolphin Park didn't have much to recommend it. Three sides of the park were twelve-foot-high hurricane fences topped with both German wire and concertina wire. Either barbed wire with two-inch spikes or barbed wire with razor blades, choose your poison, Jackie thought to herself with a wince.

McGowan looked over at her. "You okay?"

"Sure."

"Don't tell me you got sunburned too?"

"No, no, O noble red man. It's my tootsies." Jackie gingerly pulled off her canvas shoes and winced at the sight of her blistered feet. "Now I know why no one walks in Los Angeles. Those hard sidewalks are so hot they bake your feet."

"You got to get these sole inserts at Sam Sharpe's," Ral said knowledgeably. "They're filled with gel, see. Slap that sucker in the fridge-a-cooler, then you stick 'em in your peds before you move out in the morning."

"They should tell tourists these things," Jackie groaned.

"Put up signs," McGowan offered in his turn.

"Spread the word," Ral concluded.

The rest of the park abutted a senior citizens home and served as their outside recreation area. Two guards stood watching the handful of elderly men and women—mostly women—who nervously sat in a cluster around the park's one tree.

This singular vegetation, a mighty oak held together by thin, brown-painted piano wire and numerous concrete injections, had its large trunk ringed by an old wooden bench. Seated in the middle of the bench, wearing surgical scrub clothes, or perhaps just green pajamas, was a wild-haired Irish-American. The bearlike man muttered to himself and made notes, seemingly at random, on the margins of what seemed to be a seven- or eight-hundred-page typed manuscript.

Jackie turned to Ral. "Is that . . . ?"

The young man nodded. "Dat's what day say."

"Who? What?" McGowan looked up, not understanding what they were talking about.

The trio was seated, if you can call it that, near the fountain. The fountain, with a much maligned dolphin in the center, had been turned off for many years. Currently by day the fountain was a skateboard arena, at night, pieces of cardboard lined the bottom and it was used for various reclining purposes. The picnic table they were seated at, the only table left in the park, had been neatly stripped of half its top. The bereft side now featured only two cement support pillars supporting nothing at all. The bench seats on either side of the remaining half tabletop had been thoroughly torched. Park visitors therefore were left with the choice of either sitting on the intact bench and resting their arms on nothing, or resting their arms on the intact part of the tabletop and resting the rest of them on nothing.

Jackie leaned over to McGowan and informed the Lieutenant, "That man over there is C. A. Wyatt. The novelist."

McGowan gave her a blank look.

"*Cap* Wyatt . . . He was a screenwriter too. With First National before it merged with Warner Brothers. Osgood Perkins, Jack Holt, George Bancroft . . ."

McGowan shook his head uncomprehending.

"*Booze and Blood,* Michael."

"Oh, sure." McGowan had seen that one. "What a guy, hunh? That film's what, sixty years old?"

"Yes, he must be over ninety."

Ral, lying on the intact portion of the tabletop, nodded. "My pops always said Flakey Gramps over there would outlive him. Guess he was right."

Sensing that Ral would talk more freely if he wasn't there, McGowan volunteered to go find a burrito stand.

Jackie told Ral what had happened to her and what she had been told so far. She was not absolutely sure it was all right to tell the would-be cinematographer everything, but Jackie could tell that beneath the cool exterior, Ral was an intelligent and sensitive young man and that if he sensed she was holding back on him, he would resent it.

Ral, in his turn, told Jackie that he had spoken to Detective Ivie, who had come across his name in the course of checking to see if the older Ralph had credit cards. They had gotten along all right on the phone, but then the detective had sent over a thick-headed uniformed patrolman to follow up on the interview, and they had clashed so badly that Ral had refused to cooperate further.

"I take it you and your father weren't close," Jackie ventured.

"No . . . You got to understand, me and the old Ralph had worked things out. We weren't like Bill Cosby and Theo, but we stayed in touch. When he and my mother split up, things weren't too cool for a while. Things were really nowhere when he moved in with old Charo, or whatever her name was."

Jackie remembered reading about the relationship in a magazine article on Perrin that Ivie had let her read on the way to the restaurant. A man with a roving eye, as they so blithely put it in the '83 article, Ralph Perrin had settled down, more or less happily, with the Cuban-born Cara Fatima Fallangano. They had a daughter and had lived together as man and wife, although never actually marrying, for more than ten years.

McGowan returned to interrupt Jackie's woolgathering and laid down before them sodas for all, two overstuffed burritos for Ral, and an unusual dessert for the two adults to split.

"What's this?" Jackie asked, holding up the wax paper-wrapped object that looked like a lot of Cheerios fried up in some donut dough.

"We missed out on dessert at the restaurant, so I decided what the heck."

Jackie shrugged and took a bite. It wasn't bad. While she chewed, she asked, "What happened then?"

Ral shrugged. It was clear he didn't like talking about it, but figuring it was part of the price of his free lunch, he responded, "Well, my man Big Boy . . ."

"Big Boy?" McGowan asked.

"I shouldn't call him that anymore, but Pops kind of forgot that when he wasn't Joe Hollywood sometimes he had to work as the night manager at a hamburger place to pay the Man."

Jackie nodded. "Go on."

"Anyway, Pops was light-skinned, you know. And he learned to speak Spanish in the war."

"Which war?" McGowan asked.

"You know, the Spain War . . ."

"*For Whom the Bell Tolls,* Michael."

"Gotcha."

"Anyway," Ral resumed, "Pops and Charo and their kid and her family all lived in East LA and it was only when his four-eyed little pickaninny came around that he had to recall that he wasn't Xavier Cugat, you dig?"

Jackie nodded.

"Then when Pops got sick about five years ago, Charo split back to Cuba and we started to hang again. You know, not all the time, but whenever he had some bread, he'd take me out. Get me some sneaks or something. Slip me some party pennies. I liked the man. I'll miss him."

There was a moment of silence while Ral finished his drink. The old lion of Los Angeles, Cap Wyatt took advantage of the moment to leave his spot and march back to the senior citizens center, followed by the majority of his court of followers.

Jackie broke the silence by asking, "Ral, I'm sure one of the detectives has already asked you, but do you know where your father was living?"

Ral raised his eyebrows and shrugged. "Pops never really had a place after he got out of the hospital. He'd hang with his boys. He'd live in these cheap hotels. He was in this real dump on West Seventh for a while. The RE-VEL Hotel. One of these pay-by-the-week places with fruits and junkies and wacked-out vets. Some old guy runs it. He'd give vets a break. My dad was in Korea, so he could always crash there."

"Would he have maybe stashed the rest of his clothes at the RE-VEL?" McGowan asked.

"Maybe. Pops really wasn't into having a lot of things around. Especially after he came out of the hospital and Charo split with a lot of stuff he really cared about. I got like a suitcase with some old suits in it in my closet. His pal Gus probably had a lot of his crap. His merengue tapes. Shoes. Stuff like that."

McGowan took out his notebook. "Gus?"

"Gus Williams. He lives downtown somewhere. You can get his address from the union. AGVA. Gus O. Williams."

"Do you recall," Jackie asked, "if he ever mentioned my father?"

"Who's your pops? Raoul Walsh? He knew him. Said he was the best one-eyed director he ever worked for."

Jackie smiled. "Walsh is a name I picked up from my former husband. Dad's name was John Peter Costello. J. P. professionally. Pete to his friends."

"Pete Costello. No relation to Lou, right?"

"Right." Jackie smiled again.

"Yeah, I think he was one of the dudes who sued my old man."

"Actually, it was the other way around."

"Oh." Ral was quiet for a moment. "I dunno what the deal was. My old man was kinda funny about a lot of things. You know, old Ralph always thought he was being done out of something. And he probably was, at least some of the time. Pops, had . . . well, a lot of people who didn't like him. Some people thought he was a Commie. Some people thought he was a Bircher. He got slapped on 'cause he was militant,'cause he was a Tom, people didn't like who he hung with, who he slept with, who he worked for."

Ral took a deep breath. "In his day, Pops was a big guy. He'd get tanked up and beat the crap out of people. Some of 'em deserved it. Some of 'em probably didn't."

Jackie pictured the man she knew only from pictures and that one teasingly brief phone conversation.

"A few years before his stroke," Ral continued, "Pops got real wild. In and out of court all the time. Hiding from the cops. Ducking people he owed money to. He was . . . you know, he wasn't getting enough blood to the brain. I hear all kinds of stories."

Ral looked at McGowan, who guiltily finished the dessert and didn't say anything.

"Pops and me never really talked about that stuff. We talked basketball. We talked old movies. We'd sit here in the park and Pops would tell me about birds. He knew a lot about birds for some reason."

Ral stopped talking again for a few moments. Neither Jackie nor McGowan had the heart to push him. Finally, the young man resumed. "Pops came to Los Angeles in 1958. He'd done everything. He'd been in the service. He'd been a singer. He played with the all-black football teams in the thirties. Pops was an interesting guy, you know? That's one of the things I'm gonna miss about him being gone. Having some serious talks about who he was and what he really thought about things."

Jackie put her hand on Ral's shoulder. He let it stay there for a while, then slowly got to his feet. "Listen, I gotta go. I'm the bicycle deliveryman, you know. My customers await."

"I thought you were a cinematographer," McGowan commented. He regretted the question the moment he voiced it.

"I can do the job, man," Ral responded, understandably a little defensive. "I signed up with the union. But they said I may not hear from them for five years."

Jackie nodded. "I know. That's just the way it is, Ral. It's nothing against you, personally. It's a father and son union and cinematographers and camera operators last a long time. There are still plenty of people working who remember when George C. Scott was a young pup."

"That's what they tell me."

"Hey, I've got an idea!" Jackie knew she was acting impetuously, but what the heck? "Why not come to Palmer? Talk to Fred Jackson. He's a nice guy. He'll sit down with you. Look at your sample reel . . . if you have one."

"I got one."

"I can't promise you anything," Jackie continued. "But you might even be able to get some work as a TA. The college is expanding its program. They're looking to hire at least four new people. The fact you are who you are won't hurt, believe me."

"The fact I be dark brown, you mean."

"Yes," Jackie replied frankly. "And the fact that you come from a filmmaking family. You know what they say in Hollywood. The son always rises."

This drew a small smile from Ral.

"And the fact that you have some little experience working here in Los Angeles," Jackie continued. "I don't know why, but people in the Midwest are always impressed by somebody who breathed the same smog as William Wyler."

"Who's that?" McGowan asked.

"*Liberation of L.B. Jones,*" Ral responded.

McGowan nodded. He'd seen that one too.

"Think about it," Jackie urged.

Ral nodded, got on his bike, and rode off.

"Now what?" Jackie asked.

"Let's get out of this park before it gets dark and someone kills us."

The young couple ended up back in bed after all. Jackie hadn't intended for it to happen. It had started with her being offered a footrub, which she had gratefully accepted. Then it seemed only fair that she rub some more lotion on Michael's back. Then they both had to get undressed to take showers and as long as they had their clothes off anyway . . .

All of this meant that Jackie didn't get to Topanga until almost seven o'clock. As the iron doors swung open and Jackie drove the compact car the LAPD had loaned her up the driveway, she was sorry it wasn't lighter out so she could enjoy the Spanish colonial mansion of the man she had come to interview—Ronald Dunn.

When Jackie abandoned her Hyundai to walk up to the house, she noticed the front doors were open. Slowly making her way down the mansion's massive hall, with its fieldstone floors, high ceilings, and sturdy whitewashed walls, Jackie eventually came upon the man himself, seated among a covey of pillows with Hopi good-luck charms embroidered upon them. "Mr. Dunn?"

"Ms. Walsh." He gave her that sly Main Line smile. A dark-haired son of Philadelphia, Ronald Dunn had kept the good looks that had made him a heartthrob at twenty, and a leading man well into his forties. Now in his late fifties, Ronald Dunn was a little fleshier in the face, a little thicker in the waist, and his brown hair flecked with gray was probably gray hair flecked with brown dye, but Dunn still had a playboy's air and those deep chocolate-brown eyes.

"Welcome to *Cicero House,*" he said.

"Goodness."

"Not a word usually associated with me these days." Dunn swept his hand toward a small pile of scripts. "Especially when every post brings me more opportunities to play despicable villains, mostly named Roy or Steve. They said you wanted to ask me a few questions on a homicide inquiry. My suggestion, right off the top of my head, is look for the suspect named Roy or Steve."

Jackie laughed.

"Well, sit down. Do you want a drink? There's a cart down here. Help yourself. Don't be shy with the Napoleon brandy.

I don't drink much anymore, but when I do, I'm not shy."

Jackie descended the two plush steps down into the sunken living room and made her way toward the gold and marble drink cart. "Should I take off my shoes?"

"This is open-minded Hollywood. Take off everything!"

Jackie gave Dunn a half smile, filled her glass with lemon-lime seltzer and a dash of white wine, then slipped out of her shoes and sat down opposite the former television star.

"I'm surprised you don't have servants."

"Why? I'm away so much. Why pay a person thirty dollars an hour to tidy up after themselves? There's a cleaning service that comes by twice a week to dust and vacuum and clean the filters on the pool. If I'm entertaining, I can hire caterers with a lot of fresh-faced actor-slash-food servers willing and anxious to be of service. *Any* kind of service."

"You're making me blush."

Dunn pretended amazement. "Is that all it takes? You're not from Los Angeles, then?"

Jackie smiled again. "I'm from the Midwest. Palmer."

"Lovely town."

"You know it?"

"I've been everywhere. If I haven't acted there I've made personal appearances at youth clubs and shopping malls. Now with all the cable networks out there, *The Duke of Cicero* is bigger than ever. It's not a phenomenon like *Star Trek,* but there's a half-dozen conventions every year and Reichardt or I try to show up and autograph carefully licensed merchandise for obscene amounts of money."

"How is Reichardt Holm?"

Dunn waved his hand toward a framed glossy picture of his former costar. "Rickie's doing wonderfully. He has twenty or thirty blond blue-eyed children—runs a beautiful theater in Manitoba—right on the lake. He's grown a handsome captain's beard and mustache and plays Rex Harrison roles at the local celebrity summer theater for more money a week than we used to get for doing the TV show."

"Remarkable."

"We've been fortunate," Dunn responded. "I can't tell you how many people of my generation are really struggling these days. Every time I do a play or a movie I get hundreds of cards—some from people who I worshiped as a young man— begging for work. Willing to take the tiniest bit part. This is a business that turns gas station attendants into superstars and vice versa."

"I guess that brings me to the point of my visit. What can you tell me about Ralph Perrin?"

Dunn sat up alertly. "Well, here we go." Turning to his left, the film star removed a couch back cushion and pulled down a panel revealing a computer keyboard with a flat screen display monitor.

Jackie laughed. "Still a spy, eh?"

Dunn looked up, then down at the computer and laughed. "This? Oh, heavens no. This little computer setup is so rinky-dink the installer practically spit on me. My seven-year-old nephew has a better setup. This computer links by telephone lines to a computer typing service. I code key in a number and they mail off one of the four or five standard letters I send to my correspondents. The rest of the memory is taken up by my old Blacklist book and my memoirs, which I hope I never need money so bad that I have to publish. I'm searching now through both documents to see what I have on Ralph. I vaguely recall the man, although I haven't seen him for at least fifteen years, but my memory is terrible. I can't remember what exactly we worked on together. All right, here we are. Ancient history first. You know Ralph Perrin was with the Lincoln Brigade?"

Jackie took out a notebook and started making notes. "In Spain?"

"Yes."

"Communist?"

"Oh, no. These people were fighting to put a king back on the throne. Half of them were monarchists and I guess about half of them supported the anarchists."

"And he was called before the Dies Committee to testify about that?"

Dunn looked at the screen and shook his head. "No, the Dies Committee left the Lincolnists alone. Perrin didn't testify until early '53 and oddly enough he was part of Sam Wood's right-wing Americans for Americans group who volunteered to testify."

"That's people like Ward Bond and Ginger Rogers?"

"Ginger Rogers and her mother," Dunn clarified. "Bea Arthur should consider playing Lela Rogers someday. One of the great comedy parts of this century. Also Adolphe Menjou, who, it is alleged, spent the time he was allotted to testify giving the committee members clothing tips. But you wanted to know about Ralph Perrin. He testified on March 19, 1953 and again on April 27 of the same year. Then, whether or not he intended it that way, Perrin's friendly testimony got him work."

"Work that suspected Communists were fired from?" Jackie asked.

Dunn shrugged. "That sort of thing was known to happen. Anyway, Perrin was hired to work on a few of the first *My Son the Communist* pictures they were doing at that time."

"Ralph's son said he was in Korea around that time too."

"Maybe so. The credits jump around—'53, '55, '57 . . . Anyway, in early '57, Ralph Perrin was called in front of the House Un-American Committee. Mostly because of his involvement with Paul Robeson."

"They were friends?"

"Apparently they worked together on some stage show. A revue which Perrin contributed material to. He confessed to being involved with a young actress in another Broadway show. A Caucasian young woman, and for his sins he was forced to give up the names of a dozen Broadway artists who he had heard were members of the Communist Party."

"But Ralph Perrin himself was never a member of the Communist Party?"

Dunn checked his computer notes carefully, then shook his head. "Apparently not. He may have pretended to be interested and attended a meeting or two. Whether he was doing it to infiltrate the party or just to meet women is not clear from the testimony. Like with so many of the friendly witnesses, his testimony went on and off the record so much and there was so much coaching, it's difficult to tell exactly what it was he was saying. But you know what the times were then. The headlines would blare 'Perrin Names Clark in Testimony' and a career would be ruined. Perrin may have mentioned Clark's name in passing and never said a word about whether or not he was a Communist, but that was enough."

Jackie nodded. "I remember one story you told about Robert Montgomery. That the newspapers ran stories 'Montgomery Named in House Un-American Probe' and the only thing that had been said about him was that one of the witnesses used to park his car in a reserved space next to Montgomery's reserved space. And it took him years to clear his name."

Dunn turned to Jackie with a smile. "Oh, you've actually read *Unholy Allies*?"

"A wonderful book," Jackie said with a smile. "It's required for my Film History 101 class."

"That's very gratifying." Dunn beamed. "You know, this silly little book that I wrote as a hundred-page doctoral thesis has just developed a life of its own over the years. I've written six different editions of it. They even did a TV special on it."

"Did they? Oh, I'm sorry I missed it."

"Don't be. Anyway, we were talking about Ralph Perrin. Well, that's about all I have on Perrin in the book. He was very much a minor player."

"But his testifying made him enemies?"

"I'm sure it did, but everyone who testified made enemies. No matter what side they were on or what they said. That's the insidious nature of these things. People who didn't testify made enemies too. If you were a Communist and had to go before the committee and take the Fifth Amendment and suffer the blacklist for ten years while at the same time the fellow who sat next to you at all those meetings slipped through the cracks and never got called and never lost a day's work, wouldn't you hate him? If you were a John Bircher and you'd flown to Washington, D.C., to testify against the no-good sons of guns Commie unionists in the motion picture industry, but some other fellow who claimed to be as patriotic as you did nothing, wouldn't you hate that person for being a slacker? And so it goes."

Jackie took the point. "How about you, now? When did you meet Ralph Perrin?"

Dunn put the computer keyboard down and sat back. "The first time was probably in the mid-fifties. I had finally gotten to the point where I was doing some star juvenile roles with the Philadelphia Playhouse and wanted to take the next big step. I'd take the train into New York, make the rounds of the agents' offices, audition for Broadway plays, for live TV—what there was of it—and for radio dramas, which were on their last legs at that point, but there were still a lot of them around. I remember meeting Ralph while trying out for a small part on a Jack Webb program."

"Jack Webb? Really?"

"Yeah, this was when he was still working on putting together the TV *Dragnet*. He eventually had to come out here to do that. And I don't recall whether it was the radio *Dragnet* or something else, but I auditioned for Ralph and two other writers on the show—I guess they were helping out with the casting—and ended up working on shows Ralph wrote for, oh, a half-dozen times or so. He seemed like a friendly guy. A little standoffish. I guess I wasn't quite as forthcoming as I would have been if I hadn't known he was tied up with all those Sam Wood types. Like the more committed people on the other side, they tended to have a real 'you're either with us or against us' attitude. So you either spent all your spare time running to this or that American Legion Hall and contributing to dozens of right-wing causes or you just stayed clear of them altogether like I did."

"Then you met again here in Los Angeles?"

"Yes." Dunn took a sip from his glass. "Ralph probably got out here first. He may have come out with Webb. I remember hearing that he worked on the war films and then later one of the religious soaps."

"I'm surprised he was able to fit in with that crowd as a black man."

Dunn shrugged. "New York and Los Angeles weren't as bad in the late fifties for that stuff. Especially in the arts. The conservative movers and shakers were Northeast WASPs or southern California Catholics. They were probably pretty tolerant, racially speaking. A lot of them had fought with blacks in Korea. Negroes were starting to appear on college campuses, in offices, and in the theater and movies playing regular people and not just pop-eyed servants. People like Ralph Perrin, the handful of blacks who get writing, directing, or producing gigs, tended to be treated pretty well, I think. I'm talking as a white man, a black man may have a different interpretation, of course. Anyway, I ran into Ralph several times in the sixties, but we didn't work together again until 1983. It was a reunion film for Reichardt and I, which took place in Kansas City of all places."

"Kansas City?"

"Believe it or not. After nine successful years of doing espionage capers out of Chicago, Cicero County, and the greater Illinois metropolitan area, all of a sudden, here we were in Kansas City battling organized crime mob bosses. It didn't make much sense, but I guess you have to expect that these days. Ralph was one of the many writers on that project. I heard he wrote some additional dialogue for Nipsey Russell, who was in that show, and Scatman Crothers. This was right around the time Ralph went in the hospital. I sent flowers, but to be honest, I never went to see him. We talked once or twice after that. He told me he'd written a script on Marcus Garvey and that there was a good role for me—"

"A CIA man named Steve who plots Garvey's assassination?" Jackie guessed.

"Almost certainly." Dunn smiled.

"Can you tell me why anyone would have killed Mr. Perrin?"

"No," Dunn answered slowly. "That seems odd to me. You know, he never hit me up for a loan, which I probably would have given him. That's very much to his credit, by the way. With all the medical expenses he had, I'm sure Ralph was hurting. He never really called me for work. Even with the Garvey thing he wasn't asking me for a commitment to take less than my usual rate, he was just checking to see if I was interested. I never knew the man that well, but I liked him. I'm a little surprised that someone would have killed him. Especially now. You know, Ralph had the reputation of being a bit of a wild man in his early days, but he really mellowed after he got sick. It was kind of strange, you didn't know whether it was medication or he'd finally started feeling his years or whether he'd made a conscious choice to take things as they come."

Jackie paused and then blurted out, "Did you ever hear anything about him being accused of stealing a script from someone?"

Dunn took a long time before answering. "Well, Ms. Walsh, I know we're not on the record here, and normally I wouldn't comment on something like that, just because, well, you know how things are out here. You say something, just in passing, then all of a sudden it's in a headline of some supermarket magazine and the tabloid television shows get into it, and all of a sudden you've got people picketing your films. Anyway, I knew your dad, Pete."

"Oh."

"What?" Dunn gave Jackie a warm smile.

"I didn't know, you'd know . . ."

"I remember seeing pictures. Pete was very proud of his beautiful brunette daughter."

Jackie, tired as she was, felt something very nearly approaching bliss.

"I don't know quite what the situation was on *Kansas City Comeback,* Jackie, but I don't think Pete Costello would steal a script from anyone."

Jackie nodded gratefully.

"I recall, and I may be wrong about this, that Ralph was trying to buy a house up in the hills at the time. He and his wife were having some troubles and I think he thought that a nice place in Beverly Hills might make things right. He was about the age then that I am now. You would think he'd be smart enough to know that when the thing between two people isn't working, a new house isn't going to make things right."

"I agree," Jackie said simply.

"Anyway, you know what a money trap some of those places can be. I think he just got in over his head financially and was trying to bail himself out by putting the squeeze on the production company. Problem was, that was when MGM/UA was starting to come apart and your father got caught in the crossfire."

Jackie sighed. "So Ralph lost his house, and my father quit the business in disgust, and then Ralph got sick and his wife left—"

"And MGM/UA went bankrupt and the movie was a flop and Reichardt and I didn't get our new series and the people at home probably gave up TV altogether and went back to playing charades with the neighbors and reading great books."

"You have a knack for tacking a happy ending onto a story." Jackie smiled sadly.

"I can't help it." Dunn laughed gently. "I'm from the old Hollywood. So?"

"Thank you," Jackie said sincerely.

"Would you like to stay for a meal? Supper? Breakfast?"

"I have a plane to catch."

"Too bad." Dunn smiled at her.

"This really is a beautiful place," Jackie said as she climbed the steps out of the living room. "Did you ever think about getting married?"

"Think about it? No, not for a second. Actually, I've been married twice. Briefly. Miserably. And expensively divorced and when the urge to have children passed so did the urge to try that particular experiment again. It's not much fun to be lonely, but at least when I'm lonely these days it's because I'm actually alone."

"You should get a dog," Jackie suggested as they walked together down the long hall to the front door.

"I beg your pardon?"

"For companionship. My dog even solves crimes."

"How wonderful, well if you hear of a dog who can double as my agent and get me a better range of parts, keep me in mind."

"I certainly will." Jackie stood for a moment in the doorway and hoped the handsome movie star would take her hand and kiss it.

He did.

Jackie tried, but couldn't keep herself from giggling. "I've got to tell you, Ron. I'm a real sucker for this kind of thing."

Ronald Dunn looked up and gave Jackie a big wink. "You know what? So am I."

CHAPTER 13

Leaning over the top of her computer terminal to flick the on/off switch that was inconveniently located on the back of the machine, Jackie felt her sheer blouse hike up. Naturally there was someone immediately on hand in her doorway to observe it.

"Someone's getting a little sun," a voice boomed.

"Hello, Fred," Jackie replied, without having to turn around.

Fred Jackson, the cinematography instructor, fancied himself to be a sort of Hemingway character. A tall man, with crinkly blond-gray hair, bloodshot gray eyes, and a thick waxed mustache turned up at the ends like Rupert of Hentzgau, Fred Jackson was easily the most popular professor in the program and was fully aware of the fact.

"A little bird tells me," Fred practically shouted, "that you were dallying in La-La Land. Don't tell me we're about to lose our favorite scenario writetress to another television series?"

Jackie turned, looked up, and forced a smile onto her face. "No, Fred. You'll have to wait a little while longer to get your hands on this cubicle. How are you?"

"Could not be better," Fred claimed, spacing each word as if typesetting a sixteen-point newspaper headline. "Did you hear? They're finally giving me a little help. What will I do with myself if I don't have to work seventeen-hour days? I may go *mad* with boredom."

"I'm sure you'll find some hobby, Fred. Listen, have you selected your TAs yet?"

"No!" Fred boomed. "The applications are trickling in, but they're all the same basic type, Jaclyn. And I like a good mix. A good, old-fashioned—"

"Mix," Jackie supplied dutifully.

"Precisely!"

"You know, Fred, I was, as your little bird told you, in Los Angeles the last few days, doing a little consulting—"

"Feature work?"

"Cop show. Ronald Dunn's a principal, so the show may go the cable route," Jackie answered glibly.

"Ron Dunn!" Fred exclaimed. "Why that old reprobate. They say he's had more tail than a brontosaurus."

"The stories are legion, Fred," Jackie continued smoothly. "More to the point, I met a young cinematographer on the shoot, Ral Perrin, who they say has got his ticket punched for the cosmos."

"You don't mean to tell me!" Fred exclaimed again. Never much of a reader, Fred usually had to keep abreast of what was happening in his own field from the gossip he picked up around the Faculty Lounge.

"Comer of the Year!" Jackie averred. She could play Fred Jackson like no one on campus. "You know the name, of course?"

Fred's big face cranked itself into a manly wink. "Not a whole heckuvalot escapes old Fred."

"I've heard that said." Jackie smiled. "Anyway, he was bemoaning the state of affairs out there and I heard, in his voice, Fred, just the tiniest hint that he was ready for a change."

"You don't say!" Fred boomed, clearly with no clue as to what was coming.

"I think, and this would be the coup of the year if you could manage it, that young Ral may be looking to chill out for a year and do some instructing."

"Oh."

"And being such a talented young *black* cinematographer," Jackie emphasized, "and all, I told him that if he was going to take the plunge, academically speaking, he should start at the top."

"Cardiff at U Conn?" Jackson asked, by now totally confused.

"No. You, Fred."

"Of course!"

"I'll send him by, then?"

"By all means!" Now Fred was getting it.

"I can't guarantee he'll come here, though. He'll take some persuading."

"Don't worry, Jackie," the cinematography instructor reassured, "when Fred Jackson twists an arm, it stays twisted."

"You really are terrific," Jackie said, with a smidgeon of sincerity.

"Famous for it."

Jackie scooted past Fred and asked as she locked her door, "Do you know where Keith Monahan is, Fred?"

Jackson consulted a pocket watch big enough to qualify him for railroad conductor work. "On the air, or just about."

"Thank you!" Jackie rushed off. Since she obviously couldn't talk to the Rodgers radio instructor while he was on the air, Jackie stopped into the chairman's office.

A very pretty, very young secretary with her dark hair sprayed back in such a way as to make her look like a Warner Brothers cartoon skunk looked up at her from behind a big stack of new manila file folders.

"Excuse me," Jackie began.

"Hi. I'm Amy," the girl chirped.

"Is Mr. Kersch in?"

"Mr. Jonathan Kersch?" Amy distinguished carefully.

"Yes."

"No." Amy sorted through some folders in the top of a Xerox box to her left. She came up with a neatly lettered

"Jonathan Kersch, July 3" and looked inside. "Mr. Kersch is at lunch."

"Is he available for a few moments this afternoon?"

"I'll check," Amy threatened. She looked through her folders for a moment and came up with another folder labeled "Appointments, July 3." "No," Amy answered slowly, trying to make sense of her own note. "Mr. Kersch has an appointment at one-thirty P.M. with . . . She didn't leave her name." Clearly this was a bad thing as far as Amy was concerned.

"Well, I'd like to make an appointment to see Mr. Kersch for a few moments. It has to be before three o'clock, because I have a film lab at three-thirty."

"All right. I can't promise you Mr. Kersch will be available. Mr. Jonathan Kersch," Amy again clarified. "But I will put you down for two o'clock."

Jackie watched with a sort of morbid fascination as Amy moved aside a catalogue for mountaineering equipment and started labeling a new folder "Appointments, July 3" in large green letters. Finally, Jackie was able to break out of her spell and point out, "Don't you already have a folder for appointments?"

Amy stopped as if amazed and started leafing through her stack. "That's right. I do. Here it is." Amy held up the folder, then, feeling some sort of explanation was evidently necessary, she explained, "This is my first day here. I used to work for the English department where things aren't so darn busy."

Jackie left the building convinced that the world was some hellish place where incompetent office people just moved back and forth until every business, academic institution, and form of government collapsed under the weight of mislabeled manila folders, overordered paper clips, and jealously hoarded mimeograph paper nobody had used in thirty years.

Jackie cut across the campus green where a couple of students played Frisbee with a shaggy spaniel. The sight made her think, with a pang, of her own dog. Jackie promised herself she would liberate Jake and bring him home immediately after talking to Keith Monahan.

KRJD, the campus FM radio station, was housed in what had once been the college barn theater. A free-standing structure between the small faculty parking lot and the large student and visitor parking lot in the southwest corner of the campus, the Radio Arts Building was easily the saddest building owned by the university. Painted black to look more like a real building, and fed by a myriad of power lines that stretched from the taller and more modern buildings all around it, the remodelers had succeeded in transforming a humble, cheerful little amateur and summer stock theater into a building that looked like a burned-out marionette barn, held up by wires. The two-hundred-foot transmitting tower next to the barn did nothing to enhance the image.

Jackie walked inside and carefully stepped through the heavy pair of blackout curtains separating the former lobby from the former theater. She wended her way quietly through the haphazardly arranged black metal audience chairs and approached Studio One, formerly the stage of the theater. Sound studio one was now situated behind a thick floor-to-ceiling piece of DuraGlas that blocked sound from the outside only slightly and allowed no air to circulate inside the building whatsoever.

As Jackie crept toward the stage, she saw Keith Monahan seated next to the engineer at a console that had not worked very well when purchased new by a St. Louis Top Forty radio station in the late fifties. Tapping the big man on the shoulder, Jackie whispered, "Keith. May I talk to you for a moment?"

Wheezing an instruction or two to Tim, the student engineer, a stoic young lad with a beige towel affixed to his head like an extra in *Lawrence of Arabia,* Monahan then lumbered to his feet. As he moved, Monahan shook several ounces of perspiration onto the console where the salty drops hit the hot surface and sizzled like bacon grease. He then proceeded

Jackie to the back of the old barn where the offices were located. Once they got past the studio, the back area of the building was lined from floor to ceiling with electrical fans.

"Watch the power cords," Monahan warned. Jackie knew from past experience that one did have to step carefully in the radio building—black snaking power cords traversed the floor powering the coolers and soda machine necessary to keep the building's staff and students from collapsing from dehydration.

"Want a salt pill?" Monahan offered.

"I haven't been in the building that long." Jackie laughed.

"I'll be with you in a minute," Monahan promised.

Jackie turned away as the large, overweight radio instructor pulled off a Desert Shield T-shirt, once white, now a sickly and sopping yellow-gray, and replaced it with a clean blue Lake Woebegone undershirt.

"Don't worry," the big man grunted. "I don't change the gym shorts in front of people unless I've known them three years."

"Remind me to meet you at the College Rathskellar when we've known each other that long," Jackie joked.

"Hah!" Monahan responded. "If I live through the experience of working in this Turkish bath for two more years, I'll meet you anywhere you like." Monahan toweled off his arms, face, and crew-cutted scalp, then placed the towel in the hanging plastic sack where he had earlier stashed the wet T-shirt. "I'll tell you, Jackie. The day of the fat radio personality is rapidly disappearing. I have lost forty pounds since I took this job. In this atmosphere Orson Welles would have ended up playing Lincoln and Garrison Keillor would have shrunk down to the size of Baby Leroy. Step into my office."

Jackie followed Monahan into a small cubicle.

"Welcome to this historic Rodgers Barn horse stall, converted at literally no expense to the office of the chairman of Radio Studies. Excuse the smell, as you see there's no window and despite the use of every air freshener and incense known to man, you can still smell the effluvia of Trooper and Nellie and the rest of their plowhorse brethren of a hundred and fifty years ago." Monahan collapsed in a deeply stained brown wooden armchair. He then reached into a little motel-sized refrigerator near his desk and withdrew a 1.5-liter bottle of Goodwillie Good Water. He tipped it to Jackie in an unspoken offer. As soon as the film instructor declined, Monahan downed the entire bottle. "Ah!" Monahan wiped his mouth with a swash of cellulose from a roll of industrial paper towels, then leaned back with an expectant look. "To what do we owe the pleasure of a visit from such a beautiful creature to our undersea kingdom?"

"Flatterer."

"We aims to please."

"How can you stand this, Keith?"

"We're hoping for a brutal winter. What choice do we have, Jackie? Everyone gets new buildings but us. They're knocking the Engineering Building to the ground. It is sixteen years old and they're putting a new building up on the old foundation."

"They do that in Hollywood now," Jackie responded. "They call it 'Down-and-Upping.' "

"We call working in this place 'Down-and-Outing.' It's hard to believe, I admit it, but we were searching in the cellar the other day for some spare transistors and we found a splendid series of perfectly preserved cave paintings."

Jackie laughed. "You're terrible. Better keep your voice down or they'll make this place a historical landmark and you'll never get rid of it."

"Please. You're giving me gooseflesh. Speaking of down-and-upping, did you hear our guest out there? She claims some of that is going to come right here to humble Palmer town."

"Who?"

"Hanna Longmuir. And boy she's regretting coming here in that green blazer now."

"Hanna Longmuir? Really?"

"In the flesh. Melting flesh now, but that's what you get for using a nonprofit college radio station to try to plug your real estate firm. I had to bleep her four or five times. Do you know the dear lady?"

"I met her last week," Jackie replied. "At a poker game."

"Really?" Monahan's thick eyebrows shot comically skyward. "Doesn't strike me as much of a gambler. Deadly serious, our Ms. Longmuir. But she has a message the community wants to hear. Seems to think that Papa Goodwillie's money is going to trickle down to every happy home owner. And that people will be flocking here to snap up every available residence before the settlement comes through."

"What do you think about that possibility?" Jackie asked.

"Seems pretty unlikely to me," Monahan responded. "But I own a two-family home up in Robin Hill. Be great news to me if it did happen."

"Keith, I was in Los Angeles recently . . ."

"Really? You too?"

"Oh," Jackie was immediately on her guard. "You were in Los Angeles?"

"Yeah. Took advantage of the cheap fares to go to the Stan Gray shindig at the LA-AFI. They're thinking of buying an old mansion in the hills and turning it into a Museum of Television & Radio like the one they've got back East."

"Sounds like a good idea. What's your interest?"

"I'm hoping to get them to include radio in their charter, like they did in New York. I'd be willing to donate copies of a couple of hundred recordings from our archives in exchange for official recognition. It might help to call attention to the fact that we've got the largest radio program in the entire Midwest here at Rodgers. It'd be something I could take to one of Palmer's robber barons, like old man Goodwillie, and maybe talk him into contributing a couple of dollars toward a new space for us."

Jackie sympathized with Monahan but at the moment she was more interested in finding out just what he knew about the case at hand. "Keith, when you were in Los Angeles, did you happen to run into Ralph Perrin?"

Monahan's face immediately clouded over with a dark scowl. "Why would I go out of my way to talk to that jerk?"

"You know the man, then?"

"Knew him as well as I wanted to. Worked with him in New York twenty years ago. A first-class louse."

"What program was that, Keith? *Dragnet?*"

"No. Don't I wish? It was a religious program. I played the neighbor's kid who was always getting lectured by old grandpa who had a Bible story for every occasion. Not the sort of thing you'd want to revive today, but I guess it sold soap flakes in the old days."

"And you two had difficulties?" Jackie prompted.

"Perrin had been given a lot of leeway on some of Jack Webb's programs. He did a little casting, a little casting-couch casting if you ask me. He claims they occasionally asked him to direct or coach some of the actors on their readings. Knowing what a control freak Jack Webb was, I doubt it, but the producers of *The Lamp and the Way* bought Perrin's malarkey and let him stick his two cents in everywhere."

"And you didn't appreciate the way he tried to reinterpret the scripts?"

"It wasn't so much that," Monahan responded, taking a giant gulp from his second bottle. "He just had a very ham-handed acting style. He thought kids should play their roles like Andy Hardy or the East Side Kids or the Little Rascals. If you tried to play the part and react the way a normal kid would react, he thought you weren't doing enough." A buzzer then interrupted the conversation. "Yes, Will?"

The voice of the long-suffering young student engineer was heard through the speaker phone. "We're into music now, Keith. Ms. Longmuir needs a place to wash up. She has a one-thirty appointment."

"Well, point her toward the ladies' room. I'll get something for her to drink." Monahan clicked off the intercom and started to lumber to his feet. "I'm sorry, Jackie. Got to get back to the sausage factory. Did we get to talk about whatever you wanted to discuss or did we get off track completely?"

Jackie smiled and got up. "I may give you another call later in the week, Keith. But I just stopped by to chat, really."

"Well, you're always welcome," the big man said warmly. "You think of anything you want to say that may be of interest to our listeners, I'm always willing to put you on the air. Ever since we went twenty-four hours I've been tearing my hair about how to get cheap programming."

"I'll give it some thought."

"Good."

Reluctantly leaving the pungently cool office, Jackie and Monahan walked back out to the main area.

"Watch the cords," Monahan called out, seeing Hanna stumble.

"My goodness," the real estate woman gasped. "My glasses are fogged over."

"Really appreciate you putting up with the craziness and coming out today, Ms. Longmuir," Monahan continued.

"Well, it was very interesting . . ." Hanna stopped short as she saw Jackie behind the big radio instructor. "Oh, hello."

"Hi," Jackie said.

"Uh . . ." Hanna turned back to the sweaty bespectacled young Sylvie Thompson, a graduate student Jackie recognized from her own classes who was standing right next to her. "You did say there was somewhere I could freshen up?"

"Sure," Sylvie responded. "Follow me."

Jackie watched Hanna and Sylvie exit and something tickled her consciousness, way back in the furthest recesses of her brain. It slipped away again as Monahan started feeding coins into the soda machine. "Thanks again, Keith," Jackie called out, exiting.

"Anytime!"

As Jackie picked her way through the power cords and moved back out toward the front of the building she heard

Sylvie tell the radio instructor, "We've got a confirm on Kersch and Donaldson for the climbing show," and Monahan telling the young student to book them. Jackie knew that there was something she should check on, but she decided to blow off everything else in favor of calling Jason Huckle to see what happened with Jake.

CHAPTER 14

Jackie was happy. Jake was trotting alongside the reservoir slightly up ahead of her. Michael McGowan was beside her. Peter was home now, and as was so often the case after a few days away, he was actually the loving and sweet little boy she had brought into the world so many years ago. Even Jackie's three o'clock film lab had gone well. If only, she thought to herself, she could get this mystery solved and get on with her life.

"How's he doing?" McGowan asked softly.

"Good." Jackie smiled. "But if those clouds over there turn into rain, we've got to get him inside."

"He still has stuff on his coat after all the baths and dry shampoos and everything?"

"Yes. It's in his pores, Michael. It grows out with the hair."

"Jeez. How long will that keep up?"

Jackie shrugged. "Four, five months."

"Poor son of a gun. If I ever get my hands on . . ."

"Let's not talk about it."

"Sorry." McGowan turned his warm blue eyes toward Jackie's face. "How are you?"

Jackie blushed. "Good."

"When am I going to spend the night with you again?"

"I don't know. Not with Peter at home. Not for a while, anyway." Jackie then put her arm around McGowan's waist. "I do want to, though. I know I shouldn't, but I do."

McGowan put his arm around Jackie's waist as well. "If I know you're willing, then I don't mind waiting."

"Good. By the way. Jason found the report you gave him on the mace very helpful. It's not one of the bad ones, apparently."

"Good."

They carefully coordinated their walking to avoid a splintered tree trunk, then Jackie asked, "Are you going to get in trouble with your captain for using the forensics lab to solve your girlfriend's pet troubles?"

McGowan gave Jackie a warm smile. "Is that what you are? My girlfriend?"

"As long as my arm's around you."

"Well, in that case, girlfriend, I would have to say, I could care less."

"Now don't say that. I don't like reckless men."

"Don't worry," the handsome lieutenant reassured her. "First of all, we're not getting micromanaged to that degree yet. Second of all, as an old police dog, Jake gets a certain amount of professional courtesy, and third, this very likely has a bearing on the case. You know, mace lingers for a long time on human hairs as well, the lab boys tell me. I think if we do narrow this down to one or more suspects, I'm going to want to run some tests on them."

"How legal is that?"

"It's not illegal," McGowan responded. "I don't know how evidence like that would stand up in court."

Jackie nodded, then slowly withdrew her arm. "You know, Michael, I've been thinking. Maybe the person who maced Jake is not the murderer."

"What?" McGowan released his arm as well. "You're telling me that Jake got maced by some lunatic dog hater just by coincidence at the same time someone was hacking his way into your apartment?"

"No. Of course not," Jackie replied impatiently. "Obviously whoever took the chance of breaking into my apartment with me and Peter at home must have been the murderer.

Or someone close to him. But it's like you said, it happened at almost the same time. I don't think it's possible that the burglar could have gotten Jake away from the house, maced him, and then run into the studio and started hacking his way through the wall so quickly."

"But we worked this out," McGowan protested. "The entrance to the studio was on the alley, right?"

"Water Street."

"If they had that door propped open and the hammer or pick or whatever it was already set below, then . . ."

"I don't believe it, Michael. Not that fast. First of all, Jake wasn't found right beyond the fence, right? He was a good half block away almost to River Street."

"Yeah? So?"

"So he must have been at least that far away when he got maced," Jackie explained. "I mean, if he could move at all, he would have tried to come back toward the house. Especially if his assailant came back that way too."

"Okay," McGowan responded. "Let's say Jake was maced roughly where we later found him. What's wrong with that?"

"Well, the first thing is, that made the whole act visible from River Street. Joggers, people walking their dogs, bicyclists, the occasional motorist . . ."

"That part of River Street is blocked off now, except to police cruisers and emergency vehicles."

"Even worse. Don't you see? We have to believe then that the person thought that he or she could come out of a deserted house that they had no right to be in, taunt the neighbor's dog into jumping the fence, mace the dog in broad daylight—and you know how loud Jake gets when he's angry—then leave the dog in the street, rush back to the studio, run inside, and still have the energy to smash through two heavy sheets of waterproof dry wall, run into the living room of my apartment, find the manuscript, run back to the bathroom, go back through the hole, and rush out of the house to make their escape."

"Well, presumably they had a car waiting."

"It doesn't work, Michael. It really doesn't. My theory is this—the person who maced Jake came up from River Street. He, or she, was dressed as a jogger or cyclist. This way, let's say she for a moment, she would not have attracted attention to herself by coming out of a supposedly empty house."

McGowan nodded his head. "Okay, I'm with you so far."

"All right," Jackie continued, now raising her voice over the wind blowing in off the water. "Now, she probably sat down for a moment. Maybe had a drink from a water bottle, pretended to stretch out a muscle or adjust a shoe, or if she had the bicycle, pretended to fix that. When she saw the coast was clear, she took out something that she knew would provoke Jake into jumping the fence. I mean, that's the first time he's done that. He'd been barking off and on for a week because he thought he heard someone next door. Peter and I shushed him because we thought he was wrong. Now we see he probably wasn't. But a stranger, even if she was yelling at him or waving her arms wouldn't have been enough, especially if Peter was there in the backyard to call him back or calm him down. I think she used a dog whistle or something to get his attention, then did something to provoke him to attack or investigate. My guess is she had some sort of fright mask, maybe just a ski mask pulled down and that she had some sort of weapon. Maybe just a realistic-looking toy gun. A squirt gun, say, filled with bleach or ammonia. A couple of squirts with that certainly would have provoked Jake to charge. Now she would have expected Peter to come out, to follow Jake to see what he was excited about. He was about to do that when I called him back. That's why she would have stayed far enough away from the fence that Peter couldn't see her from the house. And that's why after she sprayed Jake she would have run away from the house. She would have ditched the gun or whistle or whatever it was, probably just by putting it all in a plastic bag and dumping it somewhere in the alley. She then would have run or bicycled—I like the bicycle for some reason—down to River Street. She had enough of a lead on Peter that she probably could have outraced him even if he did give immediate chase. And she would have gambled that Peter would have at least stopped with Jake for a few seconds to see what was wrong."

"So she takes off?" McGowan protested, finally able to interject his own thoughts. "Who breaks into your house then?"

"Her partner. The man. He watches her, probably from the back window in the studio. She would need that in case things went wrong with Jake or in case Peter or someone from River Street got to her before she could get away."

McGowan continued to think this through. "All right, so the male goes down, jams your phone, and hammers through your wall . . ."

"He assumes that Peter is going to be distracted for a while. Probably he's willing to mace Peter if he has to." Jackie shivered.

"What about you?"

"He doesn't know I'll be home. I usually have a lab at that time."

"Suppose he works with you at the college and he knows you're going to be home?"

"Then he knows that I'll get Peter and barricade myself into a room. It's what I did the last time. The story's gone around the campus often enough."

McGowan rubbed his chin. "You're awfully sure of all this."

"I'm not sure of any of it, Michael. Call it a hunch. It's just a feeling I get. After helping out on three different murder investigations now, I'm beginning to understand what the thinking must be."

"You should turn professional, Jackie."

Her response was an ironic half smile. "No, thanks."

"Just briefly, explain for me, why you think it's one man and one woman."

"The one who broke into my basement, I could see his glove when he pounded through my wall, and very vaguely his shape. It was a man, or a woman big enough to look like one. Also the phone-jamming toy. I'd like to shake the hand of the woman who was smart enough to bring that along."

"All right, no arguments on my end. Now explain why the outside person is a woman."

"The mace, mostly. It's the sort of compromise a woman could make."

"Compromise?"

"I think the woman, whoever she is, was, would have felt bad about taking out someone's dog. She could have been convinced of the logic of it and then the mace would have seemed like the best possible compromise. Besides, I'm sure most mace is sold to women. It makes more sense for a woman. It's light. Easy to operate, it resembles things she uses every day. It can be kept in a purse. If I were a man I'd be plenty worried carrying it around in my pants pocket. It doesn't make a noise or turn the person you use it on into a gory mess. If it does get turned on you, it's going to be a lot less hurtful than a gun or a knife . . ."

"I've got to admit," McGowan conceded. "This does all make sense."

"Of course it does," Jackie exclaimed, dropping down to her knees to hold the seated McGowan's hands, "and best of all, at the end, I'll bet you dollars to donuts that when she ran or hiked to the river, she ended up getting to their stashed car. She could drive it up to the house. He could load in all their material, and the stolen manuscript, and scrunch down so she could drive away without worrying that anyone would recognize her."

"You've convinced me, young Miss Marple. So who do we try on for suspects?"

"Well, I've got a couple. One lives close enough to where we are now to drop in and pay a surprise visit. Are you game?"

McGowan nodded.

"What about you, Jake?"

Rallying to the sound of the bugle, the old dog rose to the challenge. Once again, it seemed, the game was afoot.

CHAPTER 15

Yelena Gruber was bundling up her newspapers, deposit return bottles, and aluminum for the recycling station when Jackie and McGowan came to call.

"Oh, Jackie darling. You stopped by for a visit. You'll excuse me. I unexpected you. Come in."

Jackie and McGowan stepped into the small bungalow that the elderly Hungarian acting professor lived in and waited as she closed the door and turned up a few more lights.

"You'll excuse the disarray," she apologized, waving to the contents of her overstuffed kitchen. The small room was packed almost to bursting. Redundancy was obviously the order of the day. The same exact pots, strainers, and skillets from four or five different sets were stacked on shelves designed for narrower items and hung from pegs and bungee cords along the walls. Cookbooks, canned foods, and packages of dry goods were crowded into every available space. Clearly Yelena was the sort of woman who bought in bulk and had more than one container of sugar, flour, or tea bags open at a time. Amid all this, an enormous obese gray tabby sat on a kingly cushion atop a wooden armchair calmly eyeing the small stack of newspapers and recyclables on the floor.

"Would you like some tea?"

Jackie looked at McGowan, then gave an encouraging nod.

Yelena gave McGowan a sharp look, then pointed to a

teapot perched atop a stack of cereal boxes. "You. You look like a capable fellow. Get that kettle over there. And put some water in it. I don't like the tap. Use the bottled water in the icebox. I only have tea bags. You see what you like. Irish, English, chocolate soda pop—I have everything. I will take these things out to my car. Give us more room to have interrogations."

Noting the dubious looks her unwanted guests were giving her, Yelena assured them, "Don't worry, people. I am not fleeing to go to my secret gangster hideout. If I were ever to leave this house without Naghavasky there, he would drag me home like the kitten in his teeth. Wouldn't you, Bun-bun?"

The feline Buddha, drowsily aware that his name had been pronounced, looked around to see if anyone was preparing to serve him up a fat wriggling snack.

Yelena, in the interval, pointed to the door with her head. "Jackleen, darling. Would you get the door for me? Thank you so much. In my younger days I would have opened it with my teeth, but as one gets old one loses one's ability to do clever physical tricks. You should excuse me. I should be finished in no more than a quarter of an hour depending on how many solo trips I must make."

"May I help you, Yelena?" Jackie offered, apparently belatedly.

"So kind, darling," Yelena responded, forcing out a smile. "But you are not here on a social visit, why should you help an old lady? It is I who must help you, right? Please make yourself comfortable. Have a seat. When I come back I shall find if I have any little cakes."

Feeling more than a little bit guilty and knowing that Yelena would do nothing to get her off the hook, the moment they finished their tea and cakes Jackie sent McGowan outside to toss a stick around with Jake. Then, after stretching the amenities period to the breaking point, Jackie got to the point of her visit.

"Yelena . . ."

"Yes, darling?"

"This is about Ralph Perrin."

"Of course."

"You heard he was . . . ?"

"Almost immediately after it happened."

"It wasn't on the news, was it?"

"The Pacifica radio stations did a special on him. Keith Monahan wanted to have me on his radio station here on campus to talk about my experiences with the great man."

"Really? I just came from there."

Yelena nodded as if well aware of that fact. "This is what Communists do in the 1990s. They go on radio whenever someone from their past drops dead. Right now this is not something I want to do. Ten years from now, five years, next year, who knows?"

"What was your connection, exactly? If you don't mind me asking."

"We were lovers, dear." Yelena smiled toothily. "Why should I mind you asking? Everybody wants to know who slept with whom. It's nice that every once in a while I get to be part of the game."

"This was . . . ?"

"Many years ago. Don't ask me dates. I wouldn't have remembered then. I certainly don't remember now. I tell everyone. I keep no diaries. I keep no letters. But I'm not going to lie. I am very honest. You want to do something with me that can't be talked about, so don't do it."

"When did you last see Ralph Perrin?"

"Six months, eight months. Something like that. Funeral of a man we both knew in New York. He saw I was old. I saw he was old. We shrugged, we talked. What is there to say, really?"

"Did you talk about the hearings? About his testimony?"

Yelena shrugged. "The subject came up. The man who died, George. He never forgave Ralph. Being a very stupid man, Ralph didn't understand that. Ralph and I, we had no problems about that. Not then. Not ever."

"You forgave him?" Jackie asked, somewhat amazed.

"It is not for me to forgive. It is not for me to punish. I believe in my life everything I do, God wants me to do. When I start to do something He doesn't like, He lets me know, believe me. Ralph too must have done what God wanted him to do. If he didn't, then God punished him. God was always punishing Ralph Perrin. Me, He mostly leaves alone."

"You never felt personally betrayed?"

Yelena shrugged. "Personally? That Ralph should do this to me? Maybe I did. This kind of personal betrayal I felt many times with Ralph. Many times with many men. I never married, Jackleen. To tell you the truth, no one ever asked me. Ralph obviously felt he owed me very little. That was his right. We were never serious lovers. I was very free with my body. He was very free with his. I think we brought each other pleasure. Who knows?"

"I mean, politically."

"Darling." Yelena gave Jackie a knowing look, then started fanning herself with a cheap fan. "I am not a political person. Ralph Perrin was never a Communist. Of this I am sure. He never took any pledges not to reveal the names of his comrades. Maybe people should have been more careful discussing their business when Ralph was around. I don't know. I was never very sophisticated about keeping secrets. As you can see, I say what I think. I was an American Communist from the time I came to this country sometime in the 1940s until they made the party illegal in the late 1950s. When I came here they said, 'Become an American citizen and you have religious freedom, personal freedom, political freedom.' This seemed very strange to me. I have lived in many countries. Nowhere before have I seen a place where you have religious freedom, personal freedom, or political freedom. So I never believed it and it didn't hurt me when it wasn't true. You know who the hearings hurt? People like Ralph Perrin. He believed they'd make him a big hero. Ha. I felt sorry for him."

Jackie nodded, beginning to understand. "Did he talk to you on the telephone?"

"For what?"

"Well, to tell you he was coming to Palmer."

"Was he?"

"Yes."

"So what?" Yelena responded, reaching for a swollen devil's food cake. "I will tell you the truth, Jackleen. Most old men, you can keep them. All they want to do is complain. They think if they listen to you complain, you will let them. Me, I like young people." The Hungarian actress sucked white cream off her fingers. "Young outlooks. Maybe they are no more practical than old people, but at my age you need energy pulling you up—not complainers dragging you down. There is one old man I like, Ivor Quest. Such a handsome man. A killer, we call them in my country. Charming. Very old-world, as they say. So much improvement over the other one, 'Mr. Money Deals.' "

Jackie chuckled. "You don't like Jonathan Kersch?"

"The man is never happy. Always going up, going down. You try to talk to the man five minutes and he's buying a house and going on a trip, and meeting someone from out of town for lunch. Such a big shot. Always was he like this. In New York—same way. And what is he?—just a teacher like you and me. But Mr. Quest . . ."

Yelena waved to a framed, autographed picture of the new department chairman. "That is something else again. I wish I could kiss the fingertips of such a man. Such films he has given us. He paints with a camera, the big pictures. Love. Hope. Glory. When you sit down and talk with him, he is in your lap he is so anxious to hear what you are going to say. Never the phone calls, the letters, the telegrams, the faxes."

At that moment McGowan came back in, drenched with perspiration. "May I trouble you for a drink, Ms. Gruber?"

"Please. Have some bottled water." Yelena waved negligently in the direction of her bookcases. "They give this out now, you know, free on campus. When we needed bottled water, there was none to be had at any price. Now that the water is pure, they give it to us as gifts. I'd ask you to explain this to me, but I wouldn't understand you."

McGowan walked into the kitchen, opened the refrigerator, and pulled out a bottle of water. After a few moments of hunting, he came up with a tall, cracked glasslike item. "Mind if I use this?"

Yelena shrugged. "Why not?"

McGowan poured himself a healthy portion and started in.

"Who am I to keep a policeman from drinking from a vase?"

McGowan gave Yelena a look and Jackie had to bite her lip to keep from laughing.

"Well," McGowan replied gruffly, "did we find anything?"

Jackie smiled. "I'm not sure."

"You want to know who killed Ralph Perrin?" Yelena offered after McGowan had finished his drink and gone back out. "Well, I'll give you some advice. I think he was killed by somebody he didn't know very well."

"Why's that?" Jackie asked quietly.

"Ralph was a very difficult man. He talked tough some of the times, he acted tough some other times, which at his age was ridiculous." Yelena was quiet for a moment remembering. "And he wrote tough," she resumed. "Mr. Hard Guy. If you let him, Ralph could bully you . . . for a while. But sooner or later everyone found out that this big black man, down deep, wasn't very tough. He was pussycat, right, Naghavasky?"

The big cat couldn't be bothered to respond.

"I told you," Yelena resumed. "I felt sorry for him. All the time I know him—all the poor man ever wanted was a quiet, happy life."

When Jackie went outside into the backyard, she found McGowan and Jake playing a deadly serious game with the redundant plastic lid to a can of turpentine. The paint-removing product the plastic top had once covered had long since been disposed of, but Yelena, typically, had kept it on a shelf in a wooden bookcase next to the patio. McGowan

saw her and explained that he had started off this game by
Frisbeeing the top to Jake to run and catch. The size of the
small backyard made the run and catch aspect of the game
somewhat limited. In addition to that, after about fifteen
minutes or so, both McGowan and Jake became aware of
the indignity of putting such a distinguished old warhorse
through paces more clearly designed for a puppy. Accord-
ingly, they had changed the game. First McGowan rolled or
bounced the top into difficult places for Jake to retrieve it,
really forcing the old dog to work. Then McGowan would
have Jake lie in the little work space between the utility
shelves and the garbage cans, while he, at great length, hid
the top so that Jake could track it. Jake had just come up
with the top for the last time, celebrating the fact that he had
located it despite its being firmly enclosed by the cushions of
an old chaise lounge, when Jackie emerged.

"How did it go?" McGowan asked.

"Terrific," Jackie enthused. "How's my big beautiful
dog?"

McGowan looked at the way Jackie scratched Jake behind
his ears and felt strangely jealous. "Ready to go home?"

"One more stop," Jackie replied.

Jackie refused Jean Scott's offer of tea, both because
she had consumed so much of it with Yelena Gruber and
because she knew the book critic had work to do. After a
few moments of small talk, Jean led Jackie into her study
and gave her a thick folder of Xeroxed pages.

"This is it," Jean commented in a dry voice.

"Wow."

"It's not just stuff I had lying around the house," Jean
explained. "I work with a research service—three or four
very competent librarians making a little extra money in their
spare time. I put Mr. Perrin's name out on the wire and the
material just poured in. I haven't gone through all of it yet,
but this batch are copies, so you don't have to worry about
giving it back."

"Thank you." Jackie smiled wearily. "I don't know how long it's going to take me to read all of this. Or if I should even bother. I'm half hoping that someone might break into the house again and steal this."

"Oh, dear," Jean winced at the joke.

"I know. It's been a long day. I'm not going to get any better than that when it comes to being funny."

Jean gave Jackie a pat on the arm. "Please, dear. No need for any of that. You know, there was one thing I thought I'd show you. I wanted to tell you about it last week, the night of the poker game, but I couldn't . . . well, you'll see why."

Jackie felt a chill go through her bones. "Jean, this isn't about Ralph Perrin and my father, is it? Or my mother?"

"No," Jean replied, taking a glossy photograph out of a folder on her desk. "But it is a picture of Ralph with someone you know."

Jackie took the picture and had to study it for several moments before she recognized what she was seeing. There at a dock at a harbor-side restaurant—it may well have been Bob McHugh's Place in Marina Del Rey—was Ralph Perrin, talking to several people. None of them were immediately familiar to Jackie although she had the strong feeling they were New Hollywood executive types. One person was recognizable, however. It was a director, nearly as famous as Ivor Quest, the helmsman of a dozen major hits, mostly romantic adventure pictures or romantic comedies with Hollywood's biggest stars of the sixties and seventies. As Jackie looked at the picture of Stan Gray shaking hands with Ralph Perrin, Jackie remembered in an instant where she had last heard the name of the famous director mentioned. It had not been in connection with her film class, but in connection with raising money for a motion picture, television, and radio museum. Then and only then did Jackie recognize the tall sunglasses-obscured honey-blonde being held in a loose embrace by Ralph Perrin. It was Hanna Longmuir, standing in front of a silver and black Thunderbird and looking for all the world like a young up-and-coming starlet.

The ringing phone almost made Jackie jump out of her skin.

Jean excused herself to answer it.

Jackie quickly opened her own bundle and found, right on top, a fairly clean Xerox of the photo. A second piece of paper, right under it, bore the caption that had run below the picture. "Former Actress Hanna Long and Producer Ralph Perrin pictured here with Stanley Gray at a FILM-LA Exhibition of the director's work."

In a flash, Jackie's brain, overworked as it was, made the connections. Now the dark-haired film professor knew who killed Ralph Perrin. She knew too who maced her dog, knew who had decided the Perrin manuscript had to be stolen, and why. Unfortunately, this knowledge only made Jackie feel tired.

"Jackie?"

The weary film instructor turned to see Jean Scott standing in the doorway.

"That was for you. Lieutenant McGowan. He said to tell you that he just got a call on his cellular phone and must respond to it. He will call you at home later. Would you like me to call you a car service?"

Jackie nodded, reflexively looking out the window as if trying to see McGowan driving away. "Would you, Jean? That would be great."

Jean nodded and then cleared her throat to get Jackie's attention. "Jackie, do you know where he's going?"

Jackie turned for the answer.

"There's been another murder. It's Hanna Longmuir. They found her in the campus swimming pool."

CHAPTER 16

Jackie knew she was taking a chance doing what she did. There was no doubt in her mind that the proper course of action would have been for her to go to the Palmer Field House, where the campus gymnasium and swimming pool were located, and wait around until Michael McGowan was free to go with her.

That was not Jackie's style however, and besides—she just did not have time. Jake rode with his head out the window as Jackie's Jeep tore across town. The truth of the matter was, although Jackie was an excellent driver, the Jeep seldom achieved speeds much over seventy unless the vehicle was going down a steep hill, and Jake was used to riding in screaming police cruisers.

Without breaking a single driving rule (well, maybe a few were bent slightly) Jackie pulled into the Longacre faculty parking lot, inside twenty minutes time.

"Let's go, Jake!" she yelled. The adventurers then tore up the three stairs in front of the building and the dark-haired film instructor inserted her ID card into the building's twenty-four-hour door lock. "What do you say, boy?" Jackie couldn't resist asking. "This is a lot more fun than baking cookies, isn't it?"

Once they'd gained access to the building, Jackie made a beeline for the office of the one person she and McGowan had never got around to interviewing.

Jackie was working with her file and plasticized "Women in Film" membership card when a loud voice behind her startled a good three minutes off her lifespan.

"Well, well, well . . ."

Jackie turned with a loud "Oh" to see Marcus Baghorn, the sixtyish, loudly garbed former Broadway press flack.

"Caught in the act!" he yelled.

Jackie drew back and she heard Jake growl and go into a defensive posture.

"Easy, easy, Little Orphan Jackie. And that goes double for Big Sandy there. I'm just a harmless old kibitzer, remember?"

Jackie relaxed and took a deep breath. "Oh, Marcus. It's you."

"Who were you expecting? Al Jolson, maybe?"

"I didn't hear you walk up."

"Gum soles," Marcus explained, pointing to his feet. "My first girlfriend was an actress married to the then heavyweight champion of the world. When a man finds himself in a situation like that, he learns to come and go very quietly. What the heck are you doing? Breaking into the deputy chairman's office? Naughty, naughty."

"Blame Polly Merton," Jackie responded glibly. "She must have destroyed all the pass keys when they transferred her out of here."

"Come, come," Baghorn demurred. "Miss Amy Pummer, the new secretary, at this very moment trying on French panty hose in my office, has a wonderfully functional pass key. This turnabout is fair play, isn't it?"

Jackie stopped what she was doing to regard the motor-mouth press agent for a moment.

"Come again?"

"Last week, Johnny-boy was letting himself into your cubicle. This week you're doing it to him. What is this, practical joke time?"

"Something like that," Jackie replied. Then, bending to her task, in a few moments Jackie had the deputy chairman's door open.

Marcus, as always impervious to snubs or polite requests for privacy, followed Jackie into the office.

"Just looking at this stuff makes my back ache!" the elderly theater man announced. Jackie looked around. The source of Baghorn's comment was obvious. Everywhere in the room there were pieces of outdoor athletic equipment—plaques, badges, cups, ribbons, and full-color action pictures of Jonathan Kersch attacking nature with only his body, courage, skill, and six or seven thousand dollars' worth of expensive European equipment. Last, but not least, Jackie spotted a Spanish-coin money clip next to the desk phone.

Jackie crossed immediately to the deputy chairman's desk.

"Now what?" Marcus demanded nosily. "Gonna put a pop-out snake in one of his drawers?"

"Something like that," Jackie grimly replied. "I wish I had a real snake to leave for our deputy chairman. Have you met my mother's snake, Marcus?"

The old raconteur, anticipating a dirty joke, leered, "No—is this a *big* snake?"

"Huge," Jackie confirmed. Then, after prying open the middle drawer of the desk with a piton-shaped letter opener, Jackie managed to break the locks that held the rest of the drawers closed. The first drawer she hit on the way down yielded gold. "Like this hammer, Marcus?" Jackie asked, holding up a thin-headed blue metal hammer still exhibiting traces of plaster.

"Very nice," Marcus commented. "Me, I like a hammer with the head the size of a beer coaster. With my bad eyes and worse coordination, I'm taking no chances with my thumbs."

Jackie then held up what looked like a flare pistol. "Do you know what this is?"

"Some sort of tear gas gun?" the publicist guessed.

"Close. It shoots mace. I owe the late Hanna Longmuir an apology. It looks like it was the man who maced my dog after all."

By now most of Marcus's bonhomie had oozed away and

the elderly publicist was clearly starting to think about how this would look if the deputy chairman or a security guard happened to come along about now. "Uh, Jackie, sweetheart. A prank's a prank, girl—but maybe we should think about . . . ?"

Jackie took a Polaroid Instamatic out of her shoulder bag. "Marcus, I want you to take this photo . . ."

The flash went off and Marcus, although he was not in the shot, reflexively adjusted his bow tie.

"And bring it over to the Field House. Ask for Lieutenant Michael McGowan and then put it into his hands."

"Lieutenant Michael McGowan. All right. Who's he? ROTC?"

"Homicide," Jackie informed the publicist with a dirty look. "A woman was killed here on campus this evening. I don't know whether you knew her or not—Hanna Longmuir was her name. She worked for FutureLand."

Marcus nodded his head, jerkily. "Miss Future. Of course. Too bad. Always when I saw her waiting for Big Jon, she would try to sell me something. I told her, 'Lady, when a man gets to my age, he doesn't worry about his future. You're lucky if you can keep him from spending all his time thinking about his past.' Hell, you're lucky if you can get him to keep his fly buttoned and not drool all over himself at meals."

Jackie quickly approached Marcus. "So, you saw Hanna and Jonathan together as a couple?"

"Of course!" The publicist shrugged. "It was such a big secret?"

Jackie bit her lip and thought for a moment. "I guess I should have talked to you last week, Marcus. Now it's too late."

"That's exactly what I always tell people. Don't wait. Every minute you delay, a show dies a little death. Of course, it's different with people. A Broadway show dies, people lose money, but they can still go on. A person loses his life . . . well, if he still goes on after that . . . that's news."

Jackie opened another drawer and started sorting through maps. "Marcus, Jonathan's a climber, right?"

"All his life. He walked over a lot of people to get where he wanted to go. Which wasn't that far, believe me."

"I do believe you," Jackie responded. "But I mean a rock climber."

"Rocks. Oh, mountains! Sure. I asked him once. 'Johnny,' I said. 'Why don't you leave those mountains alone? Why do you have to climb them?' What does he say? Of course he climbs the mountain because it is there. So I say, 'So what? If you don't climb the mountain, somebody's gonna remove it?' "

Jackie didn't bother to conceal her impatience. "Where did he go, Marcus? Do you know?"

"Where would you think?" Marcus replied. "Up in the Short Hills. Where was it, he said he liked to camp? Oh, sure. I remember. Right by the reservoir."

CHAPTER 17

Stuart Goodwillie lived in the biggest home in Palmer. The town had a half dozen or so millionaires, at least two or three of whom were as wealthy as the eccentric pharmaceuticals baron, but none of them chose to live the opulent life-style that Goodwillie considered his due.

When Jackie and McGowan were finally ushered into Castle Goodwillie, they were the last to arrive for the press conference the bottled water tycoon had suddenly called.

The butler, a large, impassive South American, ushered his master's guests into a stateroom as big as the Longacre auditorium.

"Ah," Stuart Goodwillie greeted them. "At last. The amateur detective . . . and Captain McGowan."

"Lieutenant McGowan," Michael corrected him.

The beady-eyed, balding, former billionaire looked over to his solicitor, Nate Northcote and said, "I thought you . . . ?"

McGowan and Northcote exchanged unfriendly looks, then the lieutenant explained, "My former captain, Evan Stillman, and the former commissioner, Max Greenaway, told me I was going to receive a promotion after the 'Dear Slaying' murder case. Unfortunately, they both resigned shortly thereafter and I guess the paperwork was never processed."

"A pity," Goodwillie smirked. "Wouldn't you say, Nate?"

"How awful," the slick Palmer lawyer, who had put aside much of his lucrative criminal law practice to work for

Goodwillie Industries, affirmed insincerely. Clearly there was no love lost between himself and the tall lieutenant.

Jackie, a little embarrassed to see the sparks flying between her current boyfriend and her former suitor, walked over to the long conference table where another familiar figure was ensconced. It was the Palmer medical examiner, Cosmo Gordon.

"Jackie!" he cried out happily, rising to his feet at once.

"Hello, Cosmo!" Jackie smiled shyly. "I see they've fixed you up with your usual fare."

Cosmo looked down at the dinner his host had provided for him and commented, "Well, if you're saying it has the same shape as a Juniper Tavern cheeseburger, then I agree with you. But that's about where the similarity ends. Putting aside the question of accoutrements"—Cosmo indicated with a sweep of his hand the Wedgwood china the burger sat upon, the Tiffany salt and pepper shakers, the Oneida ketchup dispenser, and the Cartier flatware eighteen-karat knife and fork—"there has not and there never will be a burger this good served to the general public. I strongly suspect that Mr. Goodwillie's chef, who rumor has it makes more each year than my entire department, simply took a first-class tenderloin steak, ran it through a hamburger grinder, and then broiled it up for me in cheeseburger form."

Jackie smiled at Cosmo, then, leaving him alone to finish his meal, she poured herself a glass of raspberry iced tea and turned back to see her invited guest, Sergeant Lavan of the LAPD.

"Would you like some tea, Sergeant?"

"Got a brew, thanks," the big man replied, holding up a bottle of beer that was almost lost in his enormous hand.

"Are you supposed to drink on duty?"

"Sure—why not? If you had my job, wouldn't you?"

Jackie didn't really know how to reply, so she changed the subject. "Do you mind if I call you by your first name?"

"Actually, I do," Lavan responded. Seeing Jackie's surprised look, he explained, "My first name is Hippolito. So of course the guys call me Hippo. I hate that."

"So you like 'Sergeant'?"

" 'Sarge' is fine. I could drive an ice cream truck and I'd still go by 'Sarge.' "

"Either that, or 'Coney.' "

"There you go."

"Where's Strausse?" Jackie asked.

"Out back. Hanging with Jake."

The dark-haired film instructor was immediately somewhat worried. "Do you think they'll get along all right?"

"They should get along fine," Lavan replied. "Straussey's in heat."

At that moment Stuart Goodwillie stood up and tapped a silver pen, engraved with the initials "SG," against a crystal goblet replica of the Goodwillie bottled water bottle.

"Ladies . . . gentlemen. May we proceed?"

Goodwillie's guests immediately stopped their conversations, dining, and drinking to give Palmer's most distinguished industrialist their full attention.

Goodwillie smiled thinly at the expected full attention from his audience. Grasping the riding-crop-like baton he used as a pointer by its ends behind his back, the philanthropist arranged himself into the same orator's position he had first chosen in elementary school in 1926 while reciting "The Boy Stood on the Burning Deck."

McGowan, standing across the room from Jackie, caught the film instructor's eye and shot her a broad wink.

"For all of those who don't know who I am," Goodwillie began, in his thin, penetrating nasal voice, "I am Stuart Goodwillie. Around or about 1904, my father, Josiah Goodwillie, moved from the Alsace-Lorraine district of what was then Germany here to Palmer. He brought with him two formulas for aniline dyes. In 1920 Father teamed up with a soap maker named Charles Falk to make dyes and soaps and other household products. When the business almost failed during the Depression, my father, who survived Mr. Falk, and my older brother Mannheim gradually took the business into the pharmaceuticals game. We've weathered a few storms in our time. Since my tenure as president of F&G Pharmaceuticals began in the fifties, I have seen the world reject phosphates, my prize cover girl who it seems was once an adult film star, and the company's logo, a young lass throwing a stick to a dog, which some band of lunatics found somehow symbolic of voodoo."

The long-time residents of Palmer, remembering that whole episode, turned away or suppressed smiles.

Goodwillie moved to stand behind his desk. "Seven months ago, my scientists discovered the error that led to the city of Palmer's water supply being contaminated. We all know the consequences of our action. I was affected as badly as anyone, being confined, as you all probably know, to a wheelchair and, in addition, exhibiting all the classic signs of senility. I am now, after all this time, able to stand before an audience and deliver a somewhat coherent presentation."

Seeing a cue to applaud, several of the invitees did so. Out of sheer politeness, Jackie touched her hands together a couple of times.

"I thought when my legal staff and myself shook hands with the new head of the city council, the capable Ms. Greenspan, last month, that the nightmare had ended . . ." Goodwillie licked his lips, clearly suppressing his all-too-evident anger. "That Goodwillie Pharmaceuticals International would continue in a scaled-down fashion run by my nephew from our offices in North Africa and that the current Palmer plant could be refashioned completely into a bottled water industry. It was my dream that I could spend my last years here in Palmer opening public works projects underwritten by Goodwillie Good Water and that I could put the inglorious past firmly behind me. That dream foundered with the death of a Mr. Ralph Perrin two weeks ago."

Goodwillie glared at the others as if holding them responsible for the existence of Ralph Perrin, then resumed. "Mr. Perrin was a gentleman with whom I was totally unacquainted. Neither I nor any of my employees had any reason to do him harm. Yet we were very nearly dragged into another scandal when it was disclosed that the man had been poisoned by the contents of a Goodwillie Good Water bottle."

"Which was later found to contain acetone," McGowan interjected.

"Probably from a container of lens cleaner that Fred Jackson reported missing to the deputy department chairman a couple of weeks ago," Jackie added. "Fortunately the memo was sent during Polly Merton's tenure or we would have never found it."

Goodwillie nodded his head at the acceptable interruptions, then continued, "If the press had gotten ahold of the new scandal and done their usual number, it probably would have killed both me and my business stone dead. Fortunately, circumstances conspired with me on this occasion. The murderer chose Los Angeles instead of Palmer as the site of the killing, hoping it would be dismissed as an accident or suicide."

"If we weren't especially sensitive about the deaths of African-Americans in our city right now," Sergeant Lavan interjected, "a less thorough investigation may have let the murderer get away."

Goodwillie nodded. "Also, fortunately, the Los Angeles press had their hands full with their post-riot coverage and the Olympics and the presidential elections, all very convenient distractions at present. So the story was buried."

The philanthropist paused to wet his throat with a swig from a silver thermos and then continued, "Not knowing that their murder scheme was already going awry, the killers proceeded with their plan. Ms. Longmuir went all over town spreading a rumor—a scandalously inaccurate rumor I might add—that the Goodwillie Trust was planning to give or invest money in certain areas of Palmer. These areas, of course, were locations where the company Ms. Longmuir works for had properties they wished to unload. Investigations are currently being undertaken to find out whether or not her partner in crime owned any property in these areas. Mr. Northcote?"

The lean, sybaritic lawyer consulted a small pad. "We've located two properties to date on the South Side where Mr. Kersch, and his climbing friend Zack Donaldson, have options to buy. Presumably, Ms. Longmuir would find a buyer for the property at a marked-up price and then Kersch would exercise his option, buy the property, and then turn it over quickly at a profit."

"Thank you, Nate. Normally," Goodwillie resumed, "the sort of undertaking Ms. Longmuir and Mr. Kersch were planning would take several years to manage before they would start seeing any real money. Particularly if they stayed within the gray area of the relevant city codes that would have made such precarious transactions legal, although generally frowned upon."

Goodwillie favored his audience with a dry smile. "You know how people are. If they aren't smart enough to take advantage of the rules, they always want to hold back people who are. In any case, something happened that made our two speculators speed up their efforts. Mr. Quest?"

Ivor Quest, soberly dressed for once in a shiny gray Italian suit, rose from his armchair. "For the last year or so, I have been raising money for the university in anticipation of coming to Palmer full-time. One of the projects I was competing with for money was being fronted by an old associate and nemesis, Stan Gray, who was looking for a mansion in the Hollywood Hills to house the proposed Museum of Film and Television. I helped out a little on an 'I'll wash your hands if you wash mine' basis and I don't know to what extent I mentioned this to Mr. Kersch, but it definitely came up in conversation. Having full access to my office, Jonathan could have easily read whatever prospectus or correspondence I may have had on the matter. And of course it was no great secret in the industry. Mr. Kersch was very much into monitoring Entertainment Electronic Mailboxes through the Rodgers computer link line access. I'm sure this sort of information is readily available if you know where to look."

Quest sat back down and Goodwillie continued his narrative. "Mr. Kersch moved immediately to take advantage of
this information. We don't know how Mr. Kersch and Ms.
Longmuir first met . . ."

"Our investigations on Ms. Longmuir's background are still
very preliminary, of course," McGowan interrupted, clearly
jumping the gun a bit with his contribution. "So far we've
found that the deceased was an avid climber and skier. We
are assuming that they had some relationship previously
which Kersch rekindled in order to get Ms. Longmuir to
help him."

"Thank you, Lieutenant," Goodwillie said loudly. "In any
event, at one point, Mr. Kersch heard that a house was
available. A house in the Hollywood Hills that would be
perfect except for one thing. The lease option to buy was held
by Ralph Perrin, a man who Mr. Kersch had worked with
many years before and with whom he had a very unpleasant
experience."

"How do we know this?" Sergeant Lavan asked, looking
up from his notebook.

"Personal testimony from Mr. Kersch himself, I'm afraid,"
Goodwillie replied. "The man came to see me several weeks
ago. Wanted to borrow some money from me. Told me why.
Offered his shares in various Palmer properties as security. I
asked him why he didn't go to a bank. He said it would take
too long. Mr. Kersch claimed he needed to move within a
week. I turned him down. Told him I'm not a lender—not
a borrower either incidentally—and that I would be needing
whatever liquid funds I had to fight against possible personal
loss lawsuits. Mr. Northcote here later checked with a couple
of the local lending institutions and found that Mr. Kersch
had been turned down for a loan."

Goodwillie turned to the dapper solicitor to amplify and
Northcote again consulted his three-inch-long leather notebook.

"Banks frown on granting loans for properties in distant
states," Northcote explained. "If your credit is very good

they occasionally make an exception. Mr. Kersch's credit is very, very bad. Apparently, our Mr. Kersch believes in living far beyond his academic salary. He has borrowed heavily against what little he actually owns, and is in really no position to exercise any of his various options to buy."

Goodwillie nodded, then continued with his own account. "Apparently having obtained some sort of option to buy Mr. Perrin's property, Mr. Kersch then ran into a stone wall as far as actually raising any money. My guess is that Ms. Longmuir put up whatever front money that was called for and then was enlisted to help Mr. Kersch sell his Palmer real estate. Mr. Monahan?"

The shambling Radio Arts professor, looking surprisingly adult in a baggy blue suit, contributed, "I guess we should thank Mr. Goodwillie for getting us all together here today to solve these crimes."

Nobody moved to do so, so Monahan quickly continued, "Anyway, Ms. Longmuir contacted me, around a week ago, about coming on the radio station to talk about Palmer real estate. I was happy to book her, since we're always desperate for guests, but it turned out to be one of the strangest interviews we'd ever run. Despite constant warnings, Ms. Longmuir did everything but tap out commercials in Morse code. When I wouldn't let her give addresses and prices over the air, she spent two hours after the interview was over trying to talk me and the kids at the station into buying those properties. I mean we're talking about a guy who's clipping coupons for fast food burgers and three skinny kids who sleep six to a dorm room and live on peanut butter sandwiches and one hot cafeteria meal a day."

Goodwillie tried for a second to relate to Monahan's circumstances, then thought to himself, *Why bother?*

"So, Mr. Monahan's point is, if I may sum it up, that Ms. Longmuir was acting desperate to get money even after Mr. Perrin was killed. Why? Lieutenant McGowan, can you fill in some of these areas for us?"

Michael McGowan, who was not all that thrilled about
this civilian, no matter how powerful, horning in on a police
investigation, consulted his own notebook. "This is what the
Palmer police and the LAPD have put together so far on Ralph
Perrin, based on a search of court records and an examination
of some of the papers that he had left with a friend. Just as
Kersch was conning Perrin on how much money he could
lay his hands on, at the same he was also being conned.

"Ralph Perrin didn't actually own anything. He apparently
found the Bowman mansion, saw that it was virtually abandoned, and petitioned the courts for a transfer of property
lease. Perrin had somehow found this property that no one
really knew about. The house was unoccupied but still filled
with clothes and furniture, and it had never officially been put
up for sale. In doing some research on the owner, Georgiana
Bowman, Perrin thought he had found a house that could be
had for the back taxes, which in this particular case wasn't
much. He therefore put in his bid. The problem was, Perrin
didn't absolutely know that he was going to be successful.
According to what we can find out, Ralph Perrin lived at
the house on and off for several months trying to run down
Georgiana Bowman or her heirs.

"Obviously a house without electricity or running water
wasn't too comfortable, so he eventually moved back into a
series of cheap hotels. But he must have shown the property
to Hanna Longmuir and acted as if he were the owner.
Perhaps he even had some official-looking papers that he
could wave around, but never actually let anyone see.

"On March of this year, Ralph Perrin bribed a clerk in
the West Los Angeles Land Affairs Bureau to talk to Ms.
Longmuir and Mr. Kersch and to tell them a story. Apparently, whatever was said, whatever bona fides were given,
Jonathan Kersch was hooked but good."

Goodwillie acknowledged the policeman's contribution
with a short nod, then resumed his own narrative. "Several
weeks ago Ralph Perrin finished a manuscript about the
woman who owned the house, Georgiana Bowman. Opinions

are divided on whose idea that was. Perrin may have come up with this on his own as a way to harass Kersch and blackmail him into giving him a teaching job on campus, or the deputy chairman may have seen this as a way he could funnel some university money to the writer while he worked on raising the rest of his stake."

"I tend to favor the latter explanation, by the way," Ivor Quest spoke up. "Our Mr. Kersch was a great one for ordering supplies or equipment for the entire department that would somehow end up solely in Jonathan's own office or home. It's one of the reasons, Ms. Merton alleges, that she became so draconian about her supply closet."

"Whatever the case," Goodwillie resumed, "the manuscript seems to have settled Mr. Perrin's fate. His involving Ms. Walsh in their affairs signaled to Mr. Kersch that their secret transactions were becoming common knowledge. Surely such a course of events would be anathema to our Mr. Kersch. He very carefully established an alibi for the date of the murder—he is the only suspect in the case to have quite so airtight an alibi, incidentally—and dispatched Ms. Longmuir to do his dirty work."

"I think we should consider," Jackie volunteered, "that Hanna may not have known quite what it was she was doing. Ever since I found out that she didn't mace Jake, I've been wondering whether maybe she wasn't set up."

Goodwillie considered the proposition for a moment. "Interesting. Well, there we have the background. Ms. Walsh, why don't you bring us up-to-date?"

Jackie stood and nervously addressed the assemblage. "When Lieutenant McGowan and I were in Los Angeles, Detective Ivie of the Los Angeles police department gave us a list of several names of people here in Palmer who knew Ralph Perrin and who may have had a reason to kill him. We were proceeding at that time under the misconception that Ralph Perrin had come to Palmer and possibly had stirred up old memories and unpleasant associations."

"Do we know now for a fact that Perrin never came to Palmer?" Sergeant Lavan asked.

"We're pretty sure now," McGowan answered. "We checked with the locksmith who installed Jackie's code-locks. He remembers talking to a woman who identified herself as Jackie over the phone and got him to tell her the code. That sounds like the work of Ms. Longmuir to us."

"Plus," Jackie added, "when I talked to the person who I thought was the desk clerk at the Merrifield Travel Inn, I hadn't yet met Hanna and didn't know her voice. It all fits. She could have had a drink at the Merrifield bar and answered the pay phone pretending to be a desk clerk. She could have easily gotten keys to the studio in my duplex under the pretense of showing it to the other customers. As a frequent traveler originally from California, Hanna would have been wise to the tricks of flying standby, renting a car under an alias, and getting to and from North Hollywood late at night without calling attention to herself. And of course she was the one who put up the money, perhaps embezzling it from her employers, to pay off Perrin."

"In addition," Goodwillie wheezed, "since we know that the acetone could only be added to the water shortly before it was going to be used, we know that there was no real reason to use a bottle of Goodwillie Good Water unless the murderer had a grudge against me, which Mr. Kersch did, and unless the murderer wanted to leave a trail back to Palmer, which apparently Ms. Longmuir did."

"I don't get that," Sergeant Lavan interjected.

"If the police got close," Jackie explained, "Hanna wanted the suspicion to go to Jon Kersch, not herself. He was hoping, of course, that we could all be persuaded to believe that Ralph Perrin was killed by an old enemy from the House Un-American Activities Committee hearing days," Jackie went on to explain. "It would have led the trail away from his real estate affairs where Hanna Longmuir would be a logical suspect."

"So," Goodwillie interrupted, "you were telling us about your investigations here in humble Palmer, Ms. Walsh."

"Well, Lieutenant McGowan did most of the investigating," Jackie pointed out. "I just saw a few people and asked a few questions. I knew my mother had nothing to do with it. She wouldn't kill anyone under any circumstances, let alone having to fly all the way to Los Angeles and back and take the chance of getting into a wrestling match with a man three times as big as she is. Yelena Gruber I eliminated for basically the same reasons. She might have plunged a knife into Ralph Perrin if he had come over to her house, but I couldn't imagine her coming up with the thousands of dollars Ralph Perrin had on him when he died. I couldn't imagine Ivor Quest getting all that ruffled over Ralph, assuming he knew him at all . . ."

The director sang out, "Thank you! That's the nicest thing anyone's said about me since I directed *The Churchill Story* in 1955."

Jackie smiled and then continued, "And basically I couldn't believe that *any* of the people who hated Ralph Perrin thirty-five years ago, like Keith Monahan, for instance, would still feel so strongly about it that they would have flown halfway across the country to murder him, when ideally they could have done it anytime in the last two decades. Besides, I noticed when I interviewed Keith that he has fair skin like Lieutenant McGowan and when he changed his shirt I could see he hadn't been out in the sun for some time."

Monahan squirmed in his chair in embarrassment.

"I didn't have any particular reason," Jackie continued, "to suspect Jonathan Kersch, but as other suspects fell away, his name kept moving higher on the list. When he kept ignoring my computer mail messages that we needed to talk, the way I would try to duck people asking me questions if I did something wrong, I grew more suspicious. He was certainly big enough and strong enough to bash his way through a wall into my house. Then, when I saw a mountaineering equipment catalogue in his mail, it all came together—where he had gotten the equipment, the snorkel mask that obscured his features—I should have caught on when my vet told me that mace was mostly advertised in survivalist magazines."

Goodwillie waited for the murmurs to quiet, then resumed speaking. "If Mr. Kersch at this point was safely ensconced in the local lockup, we could start passing around congratulatory brandies and slap ourselves on the backs until our hands blistered. Unfortunately, our good friend is not only still at large, but more dangerous than ever. Dr. Gordon?"

Cosmo stood up, cleared his throat, and read from a typed report, "Ms. Longmuir's murder did not go as smoothly as Mr. Perrin's. Apparently Mr. Kersch couldn't get access to the acetone that was used in the first murder . . ."

Ivor Quest contributed, "When I heard that Fred Jackson had complained that his lens-cleaning fluid kept disappearing on him, I ordered a lock put on the camera supply closet. I gave the new department secretary, Ms. Pummer, the key, but she was apparently dining with Mr. Baghorn when Mr. Kersch came looking for her. The current theory is that he was forced to steal some window-cleaning supplies that one of the construction men had left out instead."

"The chemical we found in Ms. Longmuir's body," Cosmo continued, "was a precipitate of ether. A substance often used to weather-seal windows. This is a very toxic poison with an alcoholic smell. I don't know whether Mr. Kersch intended Ms. Longmuir's death to look like an accident or a suicide or what, but a second-year medical student wouldn't have been fooled. The body showed distinct evidence that a stronger, taller person had held Ms. Longmuir from behind. That he tried to force a toxic liquid down her throat, burning her face in the process. That he had then clubbed her with some cotton-covered object, presumably the Goodwillie Good Water bottle they found wrapped in a towel, and finally that the murderer dropped the victim into the deep end of the swimming pool, where not surprisingly she drowned." Finished with his report, Cosmo sat back down.

Goodwillie drank deeply again from his glass, belched politely into a handkerchief, and then resumed, "The problem we are now faced with is, what will Mr. Kersch do next? He has, as many of you have heard, fled up into the Short Hills near the reservoir. We assume Kersch has survival supplies with him, he may or may not have a weapon. I received a note from Mr. Kersch telling me to airdrop him a large sum of money or he will poison the reservoir and blame it on my company."

"But that's preposterous," Cosmo Gordon protested.

"Well, this whole crude attempt to make it seem that my bottled water had somehow led to the deaths of the unfortunate Mr. Perrin or Ms. Longmuir was from the very beginning preposterous. But Mr. Kersch is either so demented as to be beyond reason, or he is clever enough to understand that any bad publicity to me at this point, however far fetched, would cripple Goodwillie beyond the point of recovery."

"So what are you saying?" McGowan asked. "That you intend to pay him?"

"Of course not," Goodwillie responded scornfully. "All questions of morality aside, if word got out that a threat as specious as this one was successful in extorting money from me, then every Tom, Dick, and Harold Q. Criminal would be lining up for their piece of the pie. What the Palmer police department and I have agreed to give Mr. Kersch is counterfeit bills, impregnated with a scent reminiscent of mace. Ms. Walsh and Sergeant Lavan will have their dogs. Lieutenant McGowan and Mr. Cruz of the Palmer police department will have conventional weapons. I will provide a helicopter and heat-seeking equipment. Mr. Monahan will provide a tape that we will broadcast over speakers into the area urging Mr. Kersch to give himself up quietly. Ms. Gruber has been kind enough to provide a taped message that is, with the help of electronic enhancement, a fairly good imitation of Ms. Longmuir. On their tape, Ms. Gruber as Ms. Longmuir claims that she is still alive and that she wants

Kersch to surrender himself. Hopefully, Mr. Monahan, she has suppressed her own thick accent?"

The radio instructor nodded confidently and the other men in the room looked impressed. Only Jackie found this twist to be rather dubious. "Are you sure that's going to work?"

"Heaven knows," Goodwillie responded. "We are simply trying, Ms. Walsh, to bring in a dangerous fugitive without causing any more deaths or assaults on Palmer's water supply. Now come, everyone. Gather around and I'll show you on the map here the starting search coordinates."

As the others crowded forward, Jackie hung back. McGowan spotted her and made his way over.

"What's wrong?"

"I don't know," Jackie confessed. "This all seems wrong."

"What?" McGowan inquired. "That Jonathan Kersch masterminded the killing of Ralph Perrin, then turned around and eliminated his accomplice?"

"No." Jackie shook her head impatiently. "I'm sure we have the right man. I'm just wondering about this rescue operation Mr. Goodwillie is organizing. It strikes me as being pretty self-glorifying. You know, like those wonderful altruistic businessmen who sent private armies into Southeast Asia to bring back MIAs. I mean, if this goes wrong—if Jonathan Kersch hurts someone else, or if he gets away or does something to the water supply, you're the one who's going to get blamed, you know. Not Stuart Goodwillie."

McGowan stopped to consider the point. As he did, Jackie could see over the Lieutenant's shoulder that Goodwillie had started to look their way.

"You're right," McGowan said finally. "Should I get Chief Healy to call the whole thing off?"

"No," Jackie responded quickly. "Just keep the controls in place. The Palmer police department can welcome the assistance of Goodwillie Industries, but it should be the police, not the bottled water baron, who should be in charge."

McGowan stared at Jackie for a long moment and then said, "I love you, Jackie. Do you know that?"

The dark-haired film instructor blushed, then looked away. "Go look at your maps. I'll go check on the dogs."

Jackie left the study, found her way through the house out back to the sculpture garden, and then found Jake and Straussey camped out by a couple of large maples. Jake came bounding over and happily received a hug and a scratch from his mistress.

"So, big guy. Ready to go track down an escaped killer?"

The veteran police dog vibrated with enthusiasm.

"Good. How are you and big mama getting along?"

Jake seemed to understand the question, turned and barked for the big mastiff to join them. Strausse, comfortable where she was, glared at Jake and then went back to her nap.

Jackie saw the disappointed look on her faithful dog's face and knew that the proud animal's feelings were hurt. She crouched down, held Jake's head and neck in an affectionate hug, and whispered to him, "This whole romance thing is confusing, isn't it?"

Jake, grateful for an understanding friend, growled that he agreed.

CHAPTER 18

Edwin Gibralter told his passengers in a loud voice that was barely audible over the whirring rotors that he had been sure that he and his Big Bell Helicopter would be returned when Goodwillie Pharmaceuticals underwent their big reorganization. After all, what use would a bottled water company have for a helicopter? As it turned out Stuart Goodwillie himself had asked Edwin to stay on.

"Used to be I'd run emergency-type drugs to the hospitals!" Edwin yelled. "That was exciting. Felt like the cavalry swooping in to save the day. The new job ain't quite so demandin'. Just romping around making sure some damn fool don't dump no fridgidator in the reservoir. Or some old tick-infested buck doesn't fall over the side and drown. Dead deers are a part o' nature same as you and me, but they don't taste too damn good in your bottled water."

Not having any real argument with that, Jackie turned to McGowan. "Michael!"

"What is it?" asked the edgy homicide lieutenant. "You see him down there?"

"Not unless he's disguised as a fifty-foot pine," Jackie replied. "Listen. Do you know what's in those bags stacked over there?" The dark-haired film instructor indicated a pallet with twenty or so brown-paper-wrapped sixty-pound sacks, held together rather loosely with a network of nylon bungee cords.

184

"No." McGowan glanced over without interest. "Something to do with F&G, I guess."

Jackie shook her head impatiently. "You heard Mr. Gibralter just now. Goodwillie is now just a bottled water company. Do those sacks look like they're full of bottles? Or water?"

"No," McGowan responded, clearly still not very interested. "Maybe it's some sort of purification crystals."

Jackie shook her head. "Goodwillie Good Water is one hundred percent natural, remember? Taste this."

Jackie held out a small amount of brown-gray powder in the palm of her hand. McGowan took a pinch, put it in his mouth, and immediately made a face.

"What the hell are you giving me? Have you turned poisoner too?"

"It's spice, Michael."

"What?!"

"Spice! Like the stuff in Indian restaurants."

"Great. Remind me not to take you out for any curry dinners real soon."

"Listen to me, Michael," Jackie said urgently. "This is serious. The note that Stuart Goodwillie supposedly got from Jonathan Kersch threatening to contaminate the water supply. Did you see it?"

"Yes," the big lieutenant answered slowly. "It was a typed note. Looked like a manual machine. Nothing very significant about it, I thought."

"Typed on a typewriter," Jackie emphasized. "You're sure of that?"

"Yes. Why?"

Jackie drew closer to Michael until they were practically cheek to cheek. "That is not the Jonathan Kersch I know. He uses a computer, Michael. He loves computers. I was at a cocktail party at his house several years ago and his place is jammed with computers. I cannot for the life of me figure out why he would even own a manual typewriter."

McGowan shrugged. "So he typed it on someone else's typewriter. Why is that a problem?"

"Because it's like something out of the movies, Michael," Jackie insisted. "It would make sense if he was trying to send some anonymous note and not have it traced back to himself. But this note purports to be from Jonathan Kersch himself. Why would he go to the trouble of finding a manual typewriter in some junk store when he's on the run from the police?"

"Okay. What's your point?"

"You know who has a manual typewriter in his house? Stuart Goodwillie. I saw it on the way in."

"What?!"

"I think you should have a talk with Mr. Goodwillie when we set down," Jackie advised.

The Bell helicopter alit gently on a butte near the southwestern edge of the Putnam reservoir.

Sergeant Lavan threw open the door, unleashed Strausse and Jake from their harnesses, and then all three of them threw themselves out the door, clearly anxious to be out of the machine. Jackie and McGowan followed more gingerly. When they got outside, they stood blinking a moment in the bright afternoon sun.

"My goodness," Jackie commented, looking at the wide expanse of thickly forested woods just west of them. "This isn't going to be easy, is it?"

McGowan pointed to some distant peaks. "Over there's Kentucky. He gets that far, we're going to have some real troubles."

A few moments later Stuart Goodwillie, flanked by Detective Felix Cruz of the Palmer police department and his own man, Carnero, strode up to them. "Well, you finally got home. I was afraid Edwin had run out of gas."

McGowan turned to his associate, a lean, strong Dominican with a lined, pockmarked face. "What's the good word, Felix?"

"No sign of him, Lieutenant," the detective sergeant responded. "Now that we got the whirlybird back, we'll start making runs with the binoculars and heat sensors. If he's camped out in the middle of the trees, we'll never find him."

"We'll find him!" Sergeant Lavan shouted. "Me and the dogs!"

"You better bring a machete," commented Carnero in a heavily accented baritone. "I don't see any pathways into that stuff. It's all virgin forest."

Lavan shrugged. "He had to get in, right? If he could get in, we can follow him."

Jackie nudged McGowan, who in turn reached for Stuart Goodwillie's arm.

"Hunh? What is this?" the millionaire said at once. Deathly afraid of germs, Stuart Goodwillie did not much like being touched.

"May I have a word with you privately, sir?"

"Of course, of course," Goodwillie responded crabbily. "No need to yank my arm out of the socket though, is there?" As the industrialist smoothed the sleeve of his new Banana Republic jacket, he barked orders to his security man. "Carnero, get the equipment ready. I'll be with you in two minutes."

McGowan nodded for Detective Cruz to go with the body-guard. At the same time, Sergeant Lavan walked off after the dogs to see if they had stumbled across any scents.

"Well?" Goodwillie demanded the moment the others were out of earshot. "What's so all-fired important? We can't sit here yakking all afternoon, you know. We lose the daylight, he'll be impossible to track down."

"Mr. Goodwillie . . . we noticed you have a pallet of paper-covered bags on your aircraft."

"So I do. What of it?"

"Mind telling me what's in those bags?" McGowan asked courteously.

"The moment you're able to give me one damn good reason for butting into my business!" Goodwillie bleated. "What's it to you what materials I happen to have stored away on my private aircraft?"

"We tasted some of the powder in those bags, Mr. Goodwillie," Jackie explained. "We found it to be a very bitter-tasting spice."

"So, don't complain to me!" Goodwillie blustered. "It'll teach you to keep your tongues off other people's property!"

"We seem to keep getting off the subject, Mr. Goodwillie," McGowan pointed out. "Just what were you intending to do with the powder? Perhaps dump a little into the reservoir to make the people think there's something wrong with the water again so they'll stock up on your bottled water?"

"I think," Jackie offered, "that his sales have been down a bit since word leaked out linking his bottled water with the poisonings. He's worried about more bad publicity and he's come up with this desperate attempt to boost the sales of his product. Or maybe he just saw a great opportunity to increase the demand for bottled water in Palmer—and blame the whole thing on Kersch. Well, Mr. Goodwillie?"

The bottled water baron drew himself up like an angry rooster. "Am I on trial now? Is that it? You two better watch yourselves. I could have your jobs with a snap of my fingers."

McGowan's only response was a narrow look. "Mr. Goodwillie. The Palmer police department appreciates your assistance in this matter. But let's make one thing perfectly clear. If so much as one teaspoon of that stuff in there finds its way into our reservoir, you are going back with me in handcuffs."

Goodwillie threw his hands in the air. "You people are mad! What could you be thinking of?"

"Come on, Goodwillie!" McGowan finally shouted back at the millionaire. "Who are you trying to kid? We caught you right in the act. Your pilot told us you hire him to keep a watch to make sure an animal doesn't fall into the reservoir. If something that small could affect the taste of the water, do you expect us to believe that you don't know what an entire pallet of concentrated spice could do?"

"How do I know you didn't plant that spice on my aircraft just to frame me?"

Jackie pushed the now sputtering McGowan aside. "Mr. Goodwillie. We know what you were going to do and all we're saying is that we're not going to let you do it."

"Why on earth," Goodwillie weakly continued to protest, "after all I went through, would I take the chance of being caught polluting the water again?"

"Well," Jackie replied, "look how well it worked out for you the first time."

All of a sudden a shout was heard. Jackie, McGowan, and Goodwillie all turned their heads to see Goodwillie's majordomo, Carnero, go down, and then pull himself to cover, an arrow in the fleshy part of his thigh.

"Get down, everyone!" McGowan yelled. "Now! Felix! Where is he?"

"Up in that row of trees," Felix yelled, pointing to a scrub knoll above and to their left.

Suddenly another arrow just missed the detective sergeant's head.

"Release the dogs!" McGowan yelled.

Jackie crawled over and unfastened Jake's collar. He immediately went bounding off.

Lavan wrestled to get Strausse's collar off and then was hit by an arrow low in his right side. "Aaagh!" he cried, sitting down.

Jackie finished releasing Strausse, then rushed to Lavan's side. "Sergeant! Are you all right?"

"Yeah." The big man nodded. "I've got my vest on underneath this sweater. The point got through just enough to scratch the heck out of me." Grasping the arrow firmly, the big sergeant pushed it through and tossed the lethal-looking object aside.

All of a sudden, the air was filled with dust and Jackie and Lavan turned to see the helicopter taking off.

McGowan jumped to his feet and yelled, "Great! Get behind him! Flush him out!"

The others watched as the big Goodwillie whirlybird, with Edwin, Carnero, and Stuart Goodwillie aboard, climbed straight up, then flew off as quickly as it could go in the opposite direction.

"Come back here, you cowards!" McGowan yelled. As he did, an arrow hit the ground several feet from where he was standing.

Dodging and weaving, the homicide lieutenant ran over to where Jackie and Lavan were crouched.

"Are you all right?" Jackie asked.

McGowan panted out an affirmative. "Now what?"

Lavan cocked an ear. "Sounds like they've got him treed."

"Good." McGowan was beginning to regain his wind. "Looks like we'll have to just sit tight until reinforcements arrive."

"I don't like that," Jackie responded.

"Neither do I," Lavan quickly seconded.

"Why not?" McGowan asked. "It'll be dark soon. He won't be able to see us and the dogs will keep him treed."

"Suppose he manages to shoot the dogs with his bow and arrow," Lavan pointed out.

"And suppose Stuart Goodwillie doesn't bother to send back reinforcements?" added Jackie. "If they don't come back for us, it's a long walk back."

"Damn!" McGowan swore. "I didn't think about that. What can we do?"

"I've got an idea!" Jackie replied. With that, she gathered up her shoulder bag and ran down the hill in a different direction.

"What the heck is she doing?" McGowan complained to the big sergeant next to him. "Is she abandoning ship too?"

"Let's hope our friend Robin Hood thinks so," Lavan replied, watching an arrow come within inches of Felix Cruz.

"And what are we supposed to do in the meantime?" McGowan demanded.

"Hang tough," Lavan replied. "Chances are he'll ignore her. He'll figure we sent her out as a distraction. If he concentrates on keeping us pinned down, it lets her do what she's going to do. If he starts worrying about her, we can move up."

McGowan looked at Lavan and unsuccessfully fought back a smile. "You're not falling for our Ms. Walsh too, are you?"

Lavan laughed, and immediately winced as it hurt his rib. "No, no. Don't worry, Lieutenant. Nothing like that. It's just her choice in pets. In my experience, big dog owners are all pretty smart. So I figure it's our duty to support each other!"

All of a sudden, the two policemen heard shouts from down below. "Michael! Sergeant! Come down! We got him!"

McGowan signaled Felix to cover them as the three men scrambled down the hill. When they got to the bottom, they found Jackie, crouched down, an arm around each of the two dogs as she held them back. On the ground, ten feet away, choking and writhing in a tall pile of weeds, was the camouflage-garbed Jonathan Kersch.

"What did you do to him?" McGowan asked. "Poison his drinking water?"

"Better than that," Jackie responded, holding up the mace pistol she had nabbed from the deputy chairman's office. "Just a taste of his own medicine. He was sneaking down the tree here trying to get off a shot at Jake and Strausse when I nailed him. He's shaken up, but he'll be all right."

Gingerly pulling at the crying, retching man's arms, McGowan and Felix Cruz managed to get the suspected murderer handcuffed.

Jackie then gently pulled back and Lavan managed to get the collars and leashes back on the two dogs. When everything was secure, and the suspect, the policemen, and the two happy canines were on their way back up the butte, Jackie slipped over and put her arms around McGowan.

"Well," the lieutenant complained. "Once again, between you and your dog you didn't leave much for me to do."

"I've got a task for you, Lieutenant," Jackie responded.

"What's that?"

"Kiss me."

The lieutenant obliged. After a moment they heard a chopping noise fill the air. "Can my kisses still move you, my dear?" McGowan asked.

Jackie laughed and broke the clinch. "Come on, Jake!" she called up the hill to her jumping, barking companion. "Here comes our ride!"

CHAPTER 19

The trial of Jonathan Kersch received far less publicity than the last three court proceedings Jackie had been involved with. For one thing, this time the defendant actually pled guilty.

In the reorganization that followed, Fred Jackson and Marcus Baghorn were given the administrative duties formerly held by Jonathan Kersch, Ral Perrin was hired as a cinematography teaching assistant, and Jackie managed to exhort from Stuart Goodwillie (some would have used another similarly spelled verb as a more appropriate description) a pledge to help finance a new Radio Arts Building.

Once again the heroine of the day, Jackie sat with her mother, Yelena Gruber, and Jean Scott at a luncheon hosted by the charming chairman of the department, Ivor Quest.

"You have such a beautiful apartment!" Yelena exulted.

"Only because I fill it with beautiful things," Quest said. "Ladies." The former director held up his champagne glass and tipped it slightly to each in turn. "No man is an island. If there is one thing I have discovered in my seventy or so years upon this planet . . ."

Quest paused for a moment to let the elder ladies give each other significant looks on how well he still looked for a man of such lofty years.

"I realize more with each passing year, what a terribly collaborative process this business of living is. No one person, whether he is directing a film, or administering an academic department, or investigating a murder, is going to be successful unless he has a great many talented, energetic, and dedicated individuals to help. Ms. Walsh here is a splendid case in point. Without her help the murder of Ralph Perrin may never have been solved. Mr. Kersch would never have been run to ground, or if he had, it may well have been a long wearying process that would have dragged the entire department down in the bargain and smeared a great many good people's names. So, thanks to you, Jackie Walsh . . ."

"And thanks to Jake," Jackie pointed out, gesturing toward the now fully recovered Alsatian, currently nibbling a plate of treats and drinking from a brimming silver bowl full of the best water money could buy.

"We begin this new era in Palmer history on a high note!"

Taking this as a definite cue, Jake then let loose with a howl that could be heard for blocks around.

"It appears," Ivor concluded, "that I am being told to end my remarks here and serve the food."

"I say," Frances Costello commented, after first taking a healthy swig from her glass, "that as long as we've got five people, somewhere along the line we should work in a little poker . . ."

Later the same afternoon, Jackie left her friends to the charms of her chairman and took the limousine that had been sent for her to a rural setting, just west of Palmer. As she alit from her car and walked up the pathway to the outdoor garden, Jackie found herself in a well-disguised rest home for the elderly. Blinking in the bright sunshine, Jackie tried to guess which of the elderly ladies seated around the fountain in the garden was once the most popular female motion picture director in the United States.

She settled for the one with the most intelligent eyes.

"Ms. Bowman? Georgiana Bowman?"

An elderly woman, dressed all in white with gold accents, looked up from her game of solitaire. "I'm Georgiana, what can I do for you?"

"I'm Jackie Walsh."

"Ah. The busybody. Well, might as well join me." Georgiana reached over, fished a sweater off a chair, and tossed it to one side. "Sit down. I don't like to look up all the time. Hurts my neck."

Jackie sat down. "I'm not taking someone's seat?"

"No," the director snapped. "That sweater's mine. Don't like people sitting next to me when I'm concentrating on my cards. Not a one of them ever has anything interesting to say. If they want to complain to someone, let them get a dog." Georgiana then cracked a smile. "You are the one with the dog, aren't you?"

"Yes, I am." Jackie returned the smile. "Would you like to meet Jake sometime?"

"No. I'm too old to be disturbing my routine just to meet someone else's dog," Georgiana responded querulously. "You can send me a snapshot, if you'd like. Send me a snapshot of the two of you. It'll go into my memory box along with *everyone* else. You should be proud. Quite a lot of interesting folks in my memory box."

"I'll bet." Jackie smiled.

"You're Pete Costello's girl, aren't you?"

Jackie looked up surprised. "You met my father?"

"I met *everyone,*" the elderly director informed her. "That woman he was married to, the one with the squint, she still alive?"

"My mother?" Jackie laughed. "Yes, she's still hanging in there."

"Well, good. You tell her Georgie sent her cordial regards." Georgiana then reached for her purse. "Don't use my maiden name like you did just now. Say Georgiana Abessmy said hello. That damn Rumanian Sergei took everything he could carry when he left me, might as well hang on to the one thing he gave me, his name." Finding what she was looking for, a package of mints, Georgiana popped one into her mouth.

"All right, I'll tell her. Thank you."

"Well, what else do you want to know?" Georgiana bit

down on her mint impatiently. "You can see I'm in the middle of something, and I like to take my nap in the sun here before they wheel us all back inside. Can't sleep in these damn damp rooms they have here. Only time you can get a little rest is when the sun's out. You'll see when you get to be my age. You're cold all the time."

"Do you want your sweater?" Jackie asked solicitously.

"After it's been on the ground? Don't be daft!"

"Sorry. Ms. Bowman . . ."

"Abesh-mee. You can't handle that, call me Georgie. I don't believe in standing on ceremony. Still be a knock-kneed girl back in Palmer if I did."

"Georgie, just one question," Jackie began.

"Please, don't start grilling me on those old films. They were half a century ago. I don't remember a damn thing."

"Just one question," Jackie insisted. "What happened? Why did you retire?"

"Why do you think?"

"You got married?"

"No, no," Georgie replied disgustedly, "I didn't marry until I was working for the War Department. And that was just so I could get a decent apartment. I stopped working because they stopped offering me work. That's simple enough, isn't it?"

"What about television?"

"What about it? I said they stopped offering me work. Television is work. I would have taken it."

"Why?"

"Oh, they had every excuse in the world." Georgiana shrugged. "Some people saw the way I dressed, in suits all the time, and spread the word I was a lesbian. Forgot completely that it was the great D. W. Griffith who told me to wear those suits if I wanted to be treated like a director instead of a tart. And they said I drank, which was a lie. Makes me sick. And a doper. Ditto. I won't take the pills they give me now for the shakes, you think I was going to start with their cocaine and heroin and their goddamn pep pills?

I knew more goddamn actresses who flushed their careers, flushed their lives down the toilets with that nonsense."

"I thought you might have been blacklisted."

"Well, I was. If you can call it that. But not for being a Communist. Oh, Christ no. When I cared about politics, some forty or fifty years ago, I was ten feet to the right of Annie Rand. No, it was nothing like that, young lady."

"What was it then?"

"Why the same thing it always is. Jealousy. Small-minded bigotry. Fools deciding that everyone that came before them must be out of touch." As Georgiana talked, more than one of the other ladies who were gathered around the fountain turned to eavesdrop.

"I came along too early for them. That's all it was. Forced them to hire me to direct by locking up Lenore Coffey and Annie and Elinor Glyn, people like that. Their favorite screenwriters who happened to be women." Georgiana's face was bright for a moment as she remembered. "I helped the ladies develop their screenplays in exchange for them insisting on giving me a chance to direct. And then I had a couple of hits."

As the sun moved behind a cloud momentarily, Georgiana's good mood started to shift. "I was lucky. I know that. Could have just as easily made a bunch of turkeys that no one would want to see. So they had to keep giving me pictures. I wouldn't turn anything down, so they couldn't suspend me. The boys all went off during the war so they needed someone to turn out their B pictures. Which I did. When the boys came back and they wouldn't put me back on A pictures where I belonged, I told them to shove it."

Jackie heard giggles from some of the other old women as Georgiana primly popped another mint into her mouth.

"I had some money put aside. Invested in real estate before it was fashionable, don't you know? Figured I could always sell the land to the studios if they kept extending their back lots, like they talked about doing." Jackie had to lean forward as Georgiana's voice started to fade. "Then I had health problems. Took out one of my lungs in '62 . . ."

"Really?"

"Do it all the time now. Did it to John Wayne. Guess I'm tougher than he is. Bad thing was, I had to stop smoking, which I still miss to this day. And that was it."

"What about your home in the hills?" Jackie called. "Why did you just walk away from it?"

"I didn't walk away from anything," Georgiana snapped. "Do you see this chair? Did you think these wheels on the side were just decorations?"

"No, I meant . . ."

"I know what you meant. Listen, young lady, you appear to be a smart young woman. I assume you spent some time researching my life, didn't you?"

"I read some of Ralph Perrin's manuscript."

"Well, spare me those lies," Georgiana said loudly. "Typical hack job. Dug a few clippings out of the library, got some old fools back in Hollywood to tell him a few stories, and figured no one would bother to contradict him. Well, I told him, *in no uncertain terms*, that if he dared to print that bull dung about me in a book I would sue him from here to Hong Kong! Why?" Georgiana eyes narrowed as she gave Jackie a shrewd look. "You work for some publisher?"

"The university where I work would love to publish a biography about you," Jackie explained. "I don't suppose you would be willing to write one?"

"If I could write, young woman, I would have never become a director. But you asked about the house. Stop jumping around." Georgiana looked around for a nurse and signaled for a glass of lemonade. "Let me answer one question before you spring another one on me. Do you remember Anthony Atkinson?"

"Of course."

"Fine actor. Once. Broadway. England. World War I hero." Georgiana received her drink from the aide and rewarded the young woman with a Susan B. Anthony dollar coin, which she plucked down on a tray. "Anyway, he was a big star, then he started doing those dreary B movies at Columbia. Played Nayland Smith in all those horrible Fu Manchu movies. I directed one of them. The one with the gorilla. Dozens of Sax Rohmer novels to choose from, and they didn't use a one of them as source material." Georgiana drank deeply and, as before with the mints, didn't bother to offer Jackie any. "Insisted on updating the stories so they didn't make any sense. Had Fu Manchu commanding the Japanese Army for chrissakes. Couldn't even understand that Fu Manchu was a Chinaman! Anyway, I don't know whether you remember or not, but Anthony Atkinson was married for quite a long time to Sonia Danilova, the writer."

"I remember, well, reading about it," Jackie responded.

"You're lucky you're too young to remember the fuss they made over them. I liked Anthony. Sonia was all right, if she wasn't reading you scenes from her latest novel. Wrote these torpid penny dreadfuls about noble Rumanians in the nineteenth century. My Sergei loved them, of course. Not a word of truth to one of them, and she must have written fifty."

Jackie smiled. "Not quite as many as that, I think."

"Well, I don't care. At any rate, they bought Edmund Stowe's place next to mine in the hills in 1937. They were good neighbors. Lots of parties, but I didn't mind, since I often worked, ate, and slept at the studio. And the Atkinsons had a little boy, Aramis. I suppose someone talked them out of d'Artagnan." Georgiana shook her head sadly, once again lost in her memories. "Such a beautiful little boy. Loved to run away and hide and make his parents and their guests come look for him. Well, one day, he fell into my swimming pool. The pool hadn't been well kept up, I had a couple of big maples that dumped their leaves in the damn thing every fall, and to make a long story short, the boy drowned."

"I'm sorry. I did hear that story."

"Well, you know how tough it was on everyone. I felt terrible. Had the damn thing drained and never used it again. Not that that did any good. The Atkinsons put up a bold front, but they moved a short time later. Then split up. By

the forties I spent most of my time in a bungalow at the
Garden of Allah. You'll remember that from West's book.
Lovely set of studio apartments, almost entirely occupied by
artists. Parking lot, now, I hear. Anyway, I loaned the house
to friends when they needed it. Bela Lugosi and one of his
wives lived there for a while. Kept it as an investment, but
the damn unlucky accident made show people want to steer
clear of it. In the fifties I made a deal with the county to take
it off my hands for back taxes."

"You mean you don't own it anymore?" asked an amazed
Jackie.

"Of course not. That eyesore is a death trap. Right on
the fire line. Right on the earthquake line. Ground water's
poisoned. You remember that lawsuit, don't you? Some lye
company buried all sorts of garbage up in the hills and of
course come the first good rain, it all washed down and poisoned all our yards. I know the Atkinson house burned down
years ago. I doubt anyone is living in the house now. Have
to be some homeless people or something, if anyone."

"So, all of Ralph Perrin's attempts to get his hands on your
house and sell it . . . ?"

"The man was a fool, Ms. Walsh. I told you that when we
started this conversation. He went up to the house, poked
around, found some of the crap I left behind, and assumed
I still owned it. Maybe he checked with the county office
and they looked at the wrong form. I don't know. Then he
checked with my late husband's people, tracked me down
here, and wanted me to sign my property over to him in
exchange for some vague promise that they would make
a movie of my life and give me a lot of money for the
option. I ignored him. Told him to go soak his head or
something." Georgiana had to raise her voice again to be
heard over the giggles of her fans. "Told the nurses to
tell him I was senile if he called again. Then he sent that
manuscript to you. Somehow this fellow Kersch found out
about it. Perhaps read a few pages. Movie people are such
snoops. Read that I was out here. Came out. Found out that
I hadn't owned the place for forty years. Realized that this

fellow Perrin was pulling a Kansas City swindle on him and murdered the idiot."

"A Kansas City swindle?"

"Right out of one of my old pictures. Heard this Mr. Kersch sent a woman to do his dirty work. That's right out of my movies too. Who says they don't reflect reality? The man was a bigger fool than this Perrin fellow."

"Why's that?" Jackie asked.

"He somehow got it into his head that they were looking for a house to buy and convert to a museum. Why even I know, and I'm out here in Siberia, that Stan Gray got involved with this whole museum nonsense just so he could unload that old house of his out on Cahuenga. You wait and see if I'm wrong. After an exhaustive search process, the committee chaired by Stanley Gray will find that the perfect house is the one he owns. He'll donate it at a fabulous tax write-off and then after a year or two he'll quit the museum completely. Weasels and charlatans. That's all they were in my day. That's all they are now. Let's get back to that book, shall we, before you start asking me a dozen other questions and make me forget what I was going to say again."

"Book?"

"You said your university would like to have a biography of me."

"Why, yes," Jackie replied, surprised once again at the sudden shift in the topic of conversation. "Very much."

"Well, I have a whole crateful of diaries from the old days. Kept a lot of papers from that time in case some son of a bitch tried to sue me. What I'm thinking"—Georgiana now leaned forward and dropped her voice slightly—"is, if you or some eager beaver young woman writer wants to do a book about me, I'm ready to cooperate."

"You are?" Jackie asked, amazed.

"Sure, why the hell not? These cards never come out right. I don't have anything to do up here. I'm sick to death of watching movies. I thought the stuff they made in my day was bad. It's unwatchable now." Georgiana swallowed as if forcing down something unpleasant. "Sure, I'll cooperate. I don't know how much I can remember of the old days. I was always a 'put it out of your mind the minute you don't need it' sort of person, but those old journals of mine will probably tell you most of the story. And you don't have to worry that I'm going to want a million dollars or something. There's nothing for me to spend money on up here and I'd just as soon donate the money to your university as give it to some stupid Rumanian in-law I've never seen."

"That would be wonderful," Jackie said simply.

"You say so."

"I just want to say, Ms. . . . Georgie, that what you did for all of us . . ."

"Please!" Georgiana cut her off. "Spare me the noble female pioneer horse crap. Would have avoided every bit of it, if I could have. All they had to do was be nice, treat me like any male director, and we would have gotten along fine. But no, they fought me every step of the way. Made everything so unpleasant, I could count on one hand the films I made that I still like, and the memories I have worth cherishing. If I had known what was coming, I probably wouldn't have done it. In fact, that's what I want you to call the damn book. 'Whatever You Do, Don't Be the First.' "

Jackie smiled. "Are you really this tough, or is it just a put-on?"

"After ninety years . . . who remembers?" Georgiana smiled. Then, reaching over stiffly, she picked up the deck of cards. "What about you?"

"What about me?"

"You feel like a game of cards? Casino? Two cents a point?"

"Sure," Jackie responded, returning the smile, "what the hell."

"Now, you're talking." Georgiana signaled to the aide again, this time holding up two fingers, indicating that she should bring a glass for her guest as well. Then, as the sun grew brighter overhead, Jackie Walsh and the first lady director of Hollywood concentrated fiercely on their game of cards.